*The U.S.
Health Care
Crisis*

THE U.S. HEALTH CARE CRISIS

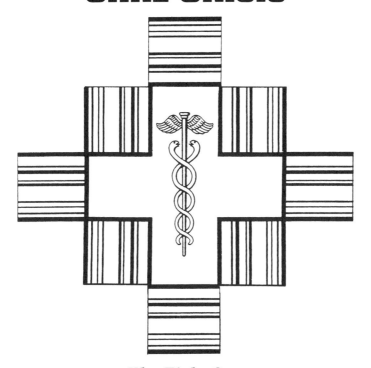

The Fight Over Access, Quality, and Cost

by Victoria Sherrow

*The Millbrook Press, Inc.
Brookfield, Connecticut*

Issue and Debate

Library of Congress Cataloging-in-Publication Data
Sherrow, Victoria.
The U.S. Health Care Crisis : the fight over access, quality, and
cost / by Victoria Sherrow.
  p. cm.—(Issue and debate)
Includes bibliographical references and index.
Summary: a discussion of how our health care system
evolved, the kind of health care now available
to American citizens, and how this care might be
improved by a cost we can afford.
ISBN 1-56294-364-2 (lib. bdg.)
1. Medical care. Cost of—United States—Juvenile literature.
2. Medical care—United States—Cost control—Juvenile literature.
3. Health services accessibility—United States—Juvenile
literature. [1. Medical care, Cost of. 2. Health services
accessibility.] I. Title. II. Series.
RA410.53.S544 1994
362.1'0973—dc20   93-51508   CIP   AC

Photographs courtesy of AP/Wide World Photos: pp. 11, 38, 42, 52, 70, 98, 113, 116, 119; Liaison International: pp. 14 (© Ronald Seymour), 66 (© Ed Malitsky); Rothco Cartoons: pp. 20 (© Tom Gibb, Altoona Mirror), 34, 88, 105 (all © Engleman); Bettmann Archive: p. 26; UPI/Bettmann: pp. 29, 57, 81; Reuters/Bettmann: p. 73.

Published by The Millbrook Press, Inc.
2 Old New Milford Road, Brookfield, Connecticut

Copyright © 1994 by Victoria Sherrow
Printed in the United States of America
All rights reserved
1 3 5 6 4 2

Contents

Chapter One
The Health Care Crisis
9

Chapter Two
*Growth of an Industry: The History
of Health Care in America*
23

Chapter Three
*The Search for Solutions:
1963 to the Present*
36

Chapter Four
*The High Cost of Health Care:
A Closer Look*
50

Chapter Five
Access and Quality
72

Chapter Six
Efforts to Control Costs
86

Chapter Seven
Models for Reform
103

Chapter Eight
Prospects for the Future
118

*Appendix 126
Source Notes 128
Bibliography 134
Index 141*

*The U.S.
Health Care
Crisis*

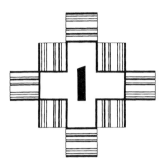

The Health Care Crisis

During the early 1800s, Thomas Jefferson said, "Without health, there is no happiness." In more recent times, a popular adage is, "If you have your health, you have everything." While many people are blessed with good health, almost everyone faces illness, injury, or disability at some point during their lives. At those times, besides the physical pain and difficulty of being unwell, there are added fears about recovering, returning to work, and the cost of the care itself. Today more than ever, people worry that a serious health problem could plunge them into poverty, for health care has become one of the most expensive commodities in America.

During the early 1990s, Americans became increasingly concerned about the high cost of health care and the way it was being delivered. By 1993, polls showed that health care was second after the economy on the list of issues that worried people most. "Becoming sick" ranked first among the fears of lower-income

Americans. The health care system was said to be in crisis. It became the subject of countless articles and television programs that described skyrocketing costs and told grim stories about Americans who were facing illness with either inadequate benefits or no health insurance at all.

As the media focused on these problems, Americans who were satisfied with their health care coverage learned about the plight of others. They saw families that had gone bankrupt or become homeless after a child was stricken with cancer or the breadwinner suffered a disabling illness. They heard about couples who divorced so that a seriously ill spouse held no joint assets. (In this way, the sick person could qualify for government aid without the family losing everything it owned.) They saw the bare refrigerators of people who needed expensive prescription drugs and had to choose between their medication and food. Many of these people were not poor or out of work; they were middle-class Americans with jobs. This led people to fear that poverty might be one severe illness or accident away.

Besides devastating individuals, the high cost of health care had serious effects on society and the economy of the United States. Government entitlements to health care (Medicaid for the indigent, or poor, and Medicare for the elderly) consumed billions of dollars a year. Although health care reform had been debated for decades, not until the early 1990s did it become a leading political issue. By 1994, seven different major health care reform bills had been proposed in Congress. People all over America engaged in an intense debate over the goals and details of health care reform.

Before the debate heated up, many Americans had not realized that the United States was the only industrial-

While President Bill Clinton proposed his concept of health care reform to Congress on September 22, 1993, he held a sample of the health security identification card that all Americans would carry if his plan for universal coverage was accepted.

ized nation in the world besides South Africa that did not guarantee some kind of health insurance to all its citizens. As of 1994, more than 37 million Americans had no insurance coverage whatsoever. Of these, 26 percent were children and 56 percent were employed but earned so little that they were called "the working poor." An additional 20 million Americans were underinsured; that is, they had some insurance but not enough to cover high out-of-pocket expenditures for any care they might want or need.

In contrast to the health insurance system in many other nations, the American system was linked to employment, although individuals and groups could also buy private insurance. Employers typically offered insurance plans as a benefit of employment and paid most of the cost, with the employee paying the rest. However, the law did not require small businesses with fewer than fifty employees to provide health benefits, and part-time workers were not generally covered, resulting in high numbers of uninsured working people. People could also lose their insurance when they were unemployed, or between jobs, or after changing jobs.

Insurance premiums had been rising yearly along with the cost of hospitalization, diagnostic tests, treatments, doctor visits, and other health care. Yet few people wanted to risk not buying insurance in view of the high cost of care and the chance of impoverishment in the event of catastrophic illness. A few days in the hospital could cost thousands of dollars, as could the fees for a relatively simple operation, such as removing an appendix or tonsils. This was more money than many people earned in a month.

Moreover, a prolonged illness could exhaust insurance benefits. Some policies set a "cap," or limit, on the amount they had to pay during the insured's lifetime. By developing a chronic condition such as AIDS or having a heart transplant or other expensive surgery, people might reach that limit. When that happened, they had to find a way to pay the costs of subsequent care themselves.

People also worried that they or someone in their family might become "uninsurable." Many insurance companies refused to cover preexisting conditions or charged such high rates for this coverage that most people could not afford it. Iowa residents Leo and Alma Patten found themselves in this situation. Mr. Patten suffered from emphysema, a lung disease, and Mrs. Patten, a diabetic, underwent heart bypass surgery in 1990. As a result, insurance companies either refused to cover them or set a cost they could not afford.

Both Pattens worked hard for years, often for businesses that closed down before they became eligible for pension benefits. They struggled to pay their bills, including costly medications, on $23,500 a year. The Pattens worried they would struggle even more after 1996, when Mr. Patten turned sixty-five, for he would no longer receive $581 a month in disability benefits from his last employer. In a letter to Hillary Rodham Clinton, whom President Bill Clinton appointed to head his Health Care Task Force, Mrs. Patten wrote, "A person keeps their nose to the grindstone, works hard, pays their bills on time. Then when your health goes bad they kick you into a corner."[1]

The working poor were often hardest hit, because they had too much income to qualify for Medicaid, and, if their jobs did not include health insurance, they could not afford to buy it on their own. Among those who had taken lower-paying jobs to get health insurance was Debra O'Connor, a single mother of three sons, one of whom required ongoing care for asthma. A former pizza

A man and woman sit in a nursing home. Many people live in fear of the terrible burden of paying for long-term care in their old age.

restaurant manager, she went to work at an aircrafts electronics factory that offered free health insurance. But as the 1990s brought federal cutbacks in defense spending, she worried about layoffs at her plant. "You can bet there's fear," said Ms. O'Connor. "I'm all for nationalized health care. If my taxes go up, they go up."[2]

As more Americans lived longer, the cost of long-term care in a nursing home or other full-time care facility was another serious concern. Neither Medicare nor most private policies covered such costs, which could be anywhere from $18,000 to more than $36,000 a year. William and Gertrude Coen of Iowa City, Iowa, were both over sixty-five. Their income of about $40,000 a year came from Social Security, income from savings, and Mr. Coen's pension from working thirty-seven years in the postal service. In 1992 the Coens spent $4,000, or 10 percent of their income, for medications and hospital insurance coverage to augment their Medicare coverage. Although insurance covered their current health care bills, they worried about needing long-term care in the future. Mr. Coen's mother suffered from Alzheimer's disease and spent seven years in a nursing home before she died, destitute. The Coens knew that such care might cost them each $30,000 a year, all presently uncovered by Medicare or their private insurance.

Part-time workers often lacked insurance. A divorced mother of two, Maria Weirather found herself in that situation. To receive care, she took a long bus ride to a city public health clinic, staffed mostly by volunteers. With barely enough money to pay her bills, she was embarrassed when she had to use food stamps. In 1990 she had surgery for ovarian cancer, at which time her ex-husband's insurance paid the bills. But he left that company, and his new job offered no health benefits. When Ms. Weirather needed more surgery, she sold her car to start paying off the $5,000 hospital bill. Relying on friends to watch her children, Ms. Weirather entered college, hoping to find a better job with insurance; meanwhile, she lived in dread of another expensive illness.

It is hard to overstate the human suffering and social ramifications of spiraling health care costs, which continue to rise at a rate exceeding the rate of inflation in the general economy. In 1992 a staggering $839 billion was spent on health care by individuals, businesses, and government. Nearly 40 percent of this involved federal payments to state governments, hospitals, physicians, dentists, and thousands of other health care professionals. One dollar out of every seven, more than is spent for food, and twice the amount spent on education and defense combined, now goes to health care. In 1993 health care was about 14 percent of the gross national product, up from 9.1 in 1980. Despite scattered efforts at controlling costs, they are still rising. By 1999, if current trends continue, the cost of health care will reach one trillion six million dollars.

Critics say that in addition to its incredible expense, the American system offers top-quality medical care only to a select group. Outstanding research has resulted in the finest medical technology in the world, and people who can pay the price often prefer to have complex surgical procedures, such as heart transplants, done here rather than in their own countries. Yet, despite spending more than any country in the world—more than $2,000 a year per capita—the U.S. system does not achieve the overall results one might expect. It ranks only twelfth in life expectancy, a too-high twenty-first in infant mortality, and twenty-fourth in the percentage of babies born with a satisfactory birth weight.

So, while spending far more than other industrialized nations, the United States does not have the best record for longevity and other indicators of health. Canada, Japan, Great Britain, and Germany spend far less per capita while providing health coverage to all citizens. In a speech on May 1, 1993, Hillary Rodham Clinton referred to these statistics, saying, "At the root of our economic and human challenge lies the fact that although we are the richest country in the world, we spend more money and take care of fewer people than many countries that are not as rich as we when it comes to health care."[3] The First Lady and others have discussed ways to improve the current health care system while maintaining what they regard as strengths—continuing scientific advances, high-quality educational programs, freedom to choose among doctors and hospitals, and widely distributed technology, for example.

High on the list of concerns is cost. The reasons for the high cost of health care in America, the subject of Chapter Four, are numerous and varied. They include inflation in the general economy, the size and many functions of hospitals, the cost of buildings, upkeep, and equipment, the cost of research and new technology, population growth, increased demand, and various social factors, such as the rising elderly population.

Other reasons can be found in the way the health care system evolved during the years, the subject of Chapter Two. For example, decades ago, health insurance only covered fees for hospital care. Physicians tended to hospitalize people more because trained staffs could help their patients, and they themselves had a better chance of being paid for their work. Hospital care is the most expensive part of the system, yet until recent years, doctors used hospitals for tests and other procedures that could be done on an outpatient basis. A lack of comprehensive "top-down" planning in the U.S. system, the free-market nature of health care, and the way in which health care is paid for have resulted in less competition, more usage, and a lack of cost controls.

Recent years have also seen an increase in the number of services insurance companies will reimburse, from forty in 1970 to about seven hundred by 1988. This happened after states enacted laws that required group insurance plans to include specific benefits. Among these added benefits were chiropractic services, catastrophic coverage, physical therapy, acupuncture, breast reconstruction after surgical removal, and such items as wigs (for hair loss from cancer treatments).

American health care has also been called inefficient and, therefore, more costly. The "system" is more a jumbled array of services produced and distributed at random. Health care payments come from public providers such as Medicare and Medicaid, nonprofit carriers such as Blue Cross and Blue Shield, and for-profit insurance companies, such as The Travelers and Mutual of Omaha, as well as individual patients. Thus paperwork—record keeping and handling and processing insurance claims—costs billions.

Health care delivery is often fragmented as well, involving many kinds of caregivers who work independently or in institutions that may be nonprofit or for profit, privately owned or government sponsored. Many people do not have a primary caregiver, such as a physician in general practice, to oversee their care. The lack of a primary caregiver can increase costs when people turn to the more expensive emergency rooms for care when they become sick. People may also develop worse conditions if they are not diagnosed and treated promptly or when they do not have sound information about ways to prevent illness or complications.

Another factor that drives up costs is that so many bills are paid by a third party (the government or insurance company). Consumers may not realize or worry about the cost of their care; they are less motivated to compare prices. Besides, most people lack the knowledge or information to judge quality and cost. Americans have high expectations and often demand the latest and best technology and treatment available. "The consumer expects more and more, the physician wants to provide more and more, and the bill gets bigger and bigger," say authors Stephen J. Williams and Sandra J. Guerra.[4]

Expensive tests and procedures add to costs. Physicians order tests that may not be strictly necessary, often to protect themselves from malpractice suits, which have increased in number and size since the 1960s. Costs have risen so high that some specialists pay annual malpractice premiums reaching into six figures.

Many people say that besides being costly and inefficient, the present system is unfair and must be changed for moral reasons. Poor people and minorities often have less access to services and may receive lower-quality care. Advocates of universal health coverage say that all citizens have a right to basic care, a subject discussed more fully in Chapter Five.

Clearly, health care reform is complex. People disagree about what to do and how to do it, and many groups have a vested interest in maintaining the current system. Because of the enormity of the task and the barriers to change, no major reforms have been enacted for several decades, although several legislators, notably Senator Edward Kennedy of Massachusetts, have proposed them.

One of the central issues for Americans in 1994 was health care. As soon as Clinton came out with a proposal to reform the system the debate began to rage.

Nonetheless, since polls show that the majority of Americans now regard health care as a citizen's right, change is inevitable. There is general agreement that the nation cannot continue on its present course. Control over health care spending is viewed as essential if America is to invest in education, the infrastructure, and industry and to compete in world markets. Increasingly, a healthier population is also seen as integral to a strong nation.

Three major targets for reform are: providing insurance coverage for all Americans; curbing and cutting costs; and improving administration, which should also reduce costs. The kind of reform that emerges after the debate will depend upon how Americans answer certain key questions such as these:

- How much should government get involved in regulating health care costs and delivery systems (for example, hospitals, clinics, nursing homes)? What role will the federal, state, and local governments play? For many people, this is critical, since they worry about government involvement in other areas of life.
- Should health insurance be based on the workplace, as now, or be handled by the government, as in most other nations? What about people (often young and healthy) who can afford health insurance but do not buy it—should they be allowed to risk the chance they will become ill, with bills so high that their costs fall on the public? Or should everyone be required to carry health insurance?
- How can costs be controlled without hindering access, choice, or quality of care? How can the administration of health care be made more efficient to reduce paperwork and other costs?

- What choices will people have in choosing health care plans and caregivers? Who decides what tests and treatments are needed?
- How much health care can be provided to everyone, considering that resources are limited? What health care services should be included in a basic benefits package? How much should it cost?
- If extra money is needed, where will it come from?
- What emphasis will be given to preventive care?
- What responsibility do individuals have for their own health care? How can consumers be better informed in judging services?

As Congress wrestled with these questions and got ready to enact a new health care plan, Hillary Rodham Clinton said, "We do not believe we have all the answers. If there are any better, more efficient, less costly, quality-driven ways of doing any of this . . . we are open to that."[5] Listening to the various reform proposals, Americans have responded with praise, criticism, concerns, or alternative ideas. The debate took on new meaning as the public prepared for historic changes in the matters of life and health.

Growth of an Industry: The History of Health Care in America

Like other aspects of life, the changing health care system reflects changes in society and the prevailing attitudes and values of the times. The history of health care is one of tremendous advances in alleviating disease and prolonging life. A closer look at that history shows how the current large, fragmented, and expensive system evolved. It points up the merits of the current system—abundant choice, rapid medical advances, minimum waiting time for routine appointments or procedures—as well as the problems with access, quality, and cost.

Ancient Roots. Attempts to prevent, identify, and cure disease have existed since ancient times, and health care was part of the early civilizations of China, Rome, Greece, and Egypt. Early ideas about protecting food and water supplies have formed the basis for today's standards of public health, which have greatly improved life in modern times.

Although earlier societies had healers and physicians, these people had few weapons against the plagues of cholera, smallpox, influenza, yellow fever, pneumonia, tuberculosis, and typhoid fever that periodically killed thousands of people. During the 1300s it is estimated that nearly half the population of Europe, Asia, and the Middle East was wiped out because of epidemics. Millions of Native Americans died after the 1400s as Europeans settled the Western Hemisphere, bringing illnesses to which they had never been exposed. Over the next few centuries, scientific knowledge in the area of health and disease slowly accumulated.

Health at the Turn of the Century. In the late 1800s, health care in America was fairly simple, and antibiotics, laser surgery, and organ transplants were hardly imaginable. Hospitals were charitable institutions where the poor could stay while sick or dying.

One or two doctors might care for a whole community, sometimes accepting as their fee for service the proverbial chicken or whatever a patient could afford. Care for most people involved a one-on-one relationship between patients and doctors, who often made house calls, and the neighborhood pharmacist. Doctors were called upon to help deliver babies, drain abscesses, set broken bones, amputate infected limbs, and, often, to provide emotional support. There were no aspirins or really effective painkillers other than the narcotic morphine. Pharmaceuticals of proven value were limited and included quinine for malaria, a vaccine to prevent smallpox, and digitalis, a plant-derived medicine, for heart disease.

As late as the 1880s, an American family might expect to lose some of its members in infancy and childhood, and women regularly died in childbirth. Tuberculosis (a lung disease that was incurable until the 1950s) was the leading cause of death. The average life expectancy for women born in 1887 was about forty-four, while today it is seventy-eight. A woman of that era who did not die before age twenty could expect to live about forty-two more years, whereas today she can look forward to fifty-eight more years.[1] If they could, people saved money in case of illness. The poor relied upon doctors who donated time to charity patients and hospitals, often sponsored by churches.

The Growth of Hospitals. As the 1900s began, changes were taking place in American health care, as it moved from the home or doctor's office to hospitals. There had been one hospital in America in 1771, but by 1900, there were four thousand. With the growth of hospitals, more better-trained nurses and other personnel were needed.

Scientific developments spurred this growth. By 1900 the germ theory developed by Louis Pasteur had ushered in the era of modern medicine. Hungarian Ignaz Semmelweis had discovered that dirty hands were responsible for childbed fever, and Joseph Lister had found ways to kill germs with antiseptics. The 1890s brought X-rays that could be used to look at bones and other organs. Then in 1900, Austrian-American Karl Landsteiner identified the four major blood groups, paving the way for blood transfusions. These, and the discovery of safe, effective anesthesia in the 1840s, made it possible for doctors and hospitals to provide many more services to patients. No longer shelters for the poor, hospitals became places where more affluent citizens sought to be healed. New wings and private rooms were built to attract paying patients. Although payments from wealthier patients soon made up most of hospital

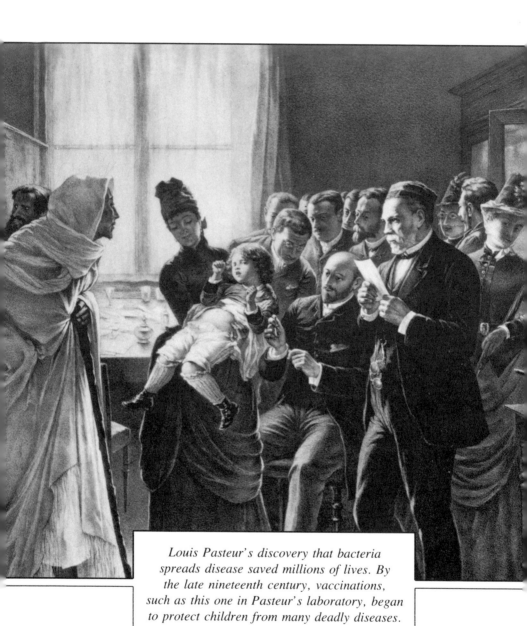

Louis Pasteur's discovery that bacteria spreads disease saved millions of lives. By the late nineteenth century, vaccinations, such as this one in Pasteur's laboratory, began to protect children from many deadly diseases.

budgets, about one third of the money came from donations.

Changing Roles for Doctors. As scientific advances continued to be made, more doctors moved from a general practice to specializing in one field of medicine. Doctors still practiced independently, although hospitals allowed them to admit and treat their private patients in return for donating services to poor patients, whom hospitals, as nonprofit institutions, had pledged to serve.

Physicians assumed more authority in running hospitals, too. Many doctors received their training by caring for patients in the hospital and in the outpatient clinics that hospitals began running for the poor. Hospitals offset some of their rising costs by offering such training to physicians and to nurses and other personnel.

New Hospital Professionals. In the early days, nursing did not require much training and was often provided free by members of religious orders, particularly the Catholic Church, which operated many hospitals. As hospitals grew and assumed more patient care functions, they required larger numbers of well-trained nurses. Besides helping physicians and giving direct patient care, nurses were expected to do managerial and clerical jobs. Hospitals set up training schools for nurses and thus continued to receive free services from student nurses. Other nurses often worked for low pay plus room and board at the training school residence. In contrast to physicians, nurses were employees of the hospital.

During the early 1900s, new personnel joined hospital staffs. Nurses' aides took over simpler tasks, such as making beds and distributing meal trays. Hospital superintendents relieved nurses of administrative duties, while clerks took over some paperwork and other clerical functions. Hospitals staffed their laboratories and X-ray departments with trained technicians. Dietitians were hired to oversee food planning and preparation. An array of other personnel joined them as time went on.

The American economy was still growing during those years, and the social reform movement led communities to set up public health departments. Concerned with public safety, they inspected water, milk, and food and established safety rules for housing and the workplace. Among the services offered were immunizations, health education, mother and infant care, and home care by visiting nurses. Care for the mentally ill was also improving, and state mental hospitals were built and staffed. After the 1920s, more women chose to have their babies in the hospital, leading hospitals and their staffs to further expand.

Rising Costs, Hard Times. As hospital costs rose, so did the patients' bills. Some funding still came from churches and community boards, and from philanthropists, often families who had made their fortune during the industrial boom of the late 1800s. Federal and state governments had little involvement beyond providing some indirect aid by exempting hospitals from certain taxes and making hospital contributions tax deductible.

As early as 1910, middle-class people were having trouble paying their medical bills. Soon, even more affluent people began to wonder if they would be able to afford hospitalization. The idea of health insurance was suggested but did not catch on until the 1930s, when the Great Depression caused massive unemployment and poverty. People became concerned not only with the cost of health care but with financial security, especially during old age. In response, President Franklin D. Roosevelt pushed for legislation in the form of the So-

It took the Great Depression to convince Americans that government aid for retired and disabled workers was a necessity. President Franklin D. Roosevelt signed the Social Security Act in 1935. Behind him stands his Secretary of Labor, Frances Perkins, a tireless advocate of the worker.

cial Security Act of 1935, a government-sponsored pension fund for the elderly and disabled.

There was also a call for universal health care during these years, something social reformers had urged for decades. Germany and some other industrialized countries already had such programs. During the 1930s, Great Britain began planning a program that would be launched as the National Health Service in 1948. But the emphasis on free enterprise and fear about government interference kept such programs from gaining wide support in the United States. Opponents worried that government regulation would lessen the quality of care and interfere with the decision making of physicians and other health care professionals. A government-run system might prevent citizens from choosing what kind of care they could receive and the people and facilities that would provide it.

The Development of Insurance. Searching for other ways to handle health care costs, Americans gravitated toward the idea of medical insurance and prepaid hospitalization plans during the 1930s. A group of 1,250 schoolteachers in Houston asked Baylor University Hospital to guarantee them a certain number of days with medical care in the hospital each year in exchange for a set monthly fee of fifty cents per person. This hospital-sponsored prepayment plan was named Blue Cross. The idea expanded to include prepayment for surgery, sponsored by medical societies and called Blue Shield.

Traditionally, insurance—called assurance—had involved a payment made to a fund in order to protect against unexpected financial loss in the event of a flood, fire, theft, or other harmful event. Individuals seldom encounter these disasters, but they occur among the larger population at fairly predictable rates—hence the idea of pooling individuals into larger groups. At the time, accident insurance was already available from commercial insurance carriers. As the cost of health care became more daunting, provisions for illness were added to these accident policies. High rates of diphtheria, polio, smallpox, scarlet fever, typhoid fever, and tuberculosis, which often required a long convalescence, made this a widespread concern.

The Blue Cross program spread across the nation, and the other program, Blue Shield, offered reimbursement of physicians' bills. Insurance, or third-party reimbursement, became the foundation of the health care payment system. Soon, insurance became job linked. During World War II, the federal government enforced wage controls, but companies were able to offer workers nonwage benefits, so labor unions pushed for health insurance as a legal nonwage benefit for American workers.

Prepaid hospital insurance had a major impact on the growing health care industry. It promoted more use of the hospital for health care. Many patients did not realize what their actual health care costs were, and physicians were more inclined to give patients as much care as might possibly help them. Medical practices, hospitals, and insurance companies all operated independently in this system, with no central planning.

Postwar Concerns. The American economy was strong after World War II ended in 1945. Hospital construction had been neglected during the Depression, and in this atmosphere of prosperity, leaders decided to deal with the hospital shortage in some parts of the nation.

Under President Harry S. Truman, Congress passed the Hill-Burton Act (or Hospital Survey and Construction Act of 1946), which included federal money and tax benefits to help communities build needed hospitals. The government did no central planning due to opposition by the American Medical Association (AMA) and by others who objected to government involvement in health care. It provided information and materials, distributed money, and set requirements for local organizations that were told to develop plans with their state governments.

Later, the act would add funding for nursing homes (1954) and by the 1970s would emphasize renovating and replacing facilities, rather than building new ones. Hill-Burton also aided facilities for outpatient care and rehabilitation. During these years, the needs of poor rural and urban areas became clearer. Government aid accounted for up to 90 percent of the funds needed for facilities in these places.

Another postwar priority was to improve mental health care at state hospitals, the subject of harsh criticism. Newspapers, books, and movies told grim stories of patients who languished in these settings for months or years, dirty and neglected, even mistreated. New therapies and medications became increasingly available after the war, making reform in this area promising. State legislators increased spending for state hospitals and education efforts aimed to help the public understand more about mental illness.

Psychiatrists and other mental health professionals learned more about the value of prevention and early treatment, and research showed that some patients improved greatly without hospitalization. The idea of promoting mental health was gaining ground in an era of rapid advances in knowledge and treatment.

Changing Attitudes. The postwar years also saw increasing public expectations. During World War II, people in the armed forces had become accustomed to better, more comprehensive health care than was typical for civilians. Military health care was highly organized with top-notch physicians, nurses, technicians, and others. Skillful coordination and use of resources enabled caregivers to perform efficiently, even under the stressful conditions of war. Combat units managed to save 96 percent of those injured in battle. Moreover, the military made a concerted effort to teach people how to stay healthy through good nutrition, fitness, sanitation, and safety measures.

Nurses and other professionals had also taken on a larger role during the war. As officers in the armed services, they had been responsible for making new decisions and carrying out more functions. Back in America, the shortage of physicians and nurses meant new personnel must be trained to assume more traditional nursing functions while nurses became more highly trained and specialized. Advances in medical science expedited this trend.

With the Hill-Burton Act and heightened interest in serving poorer Americans, state and federal governments took a more active role. The government encouraged insurance plans by giving employers tax exemptions for payments toward employee insurance. Employees were required to enroll in these plans.

By 1952 more than half of all Americans had health insurance coverage, primarily medical care that involved hospitalization. Hospitals were reimbursed on the basis of their costs, in cooperation with the insurance companies. As before, doctors set their own fees. Visits to doctors and hospitals increased greatly during the postwar years, supported by a healthy economy that benefited from a trade surplus and no federal deficit.

Debates Over the Role of Government. In 1946, his second year in office, President Truman developed a

"I'm not in favor of any health plan that doesn't cover Vet bills."

What and who should be covered has been an issue ever since health insurance first came into being.

plan for national health insurance that would cover all Americans. The idea was not new, having been discussed off and on since the early 1900s. During the 1930s, the Committee on the Costs of Medical Care was formed by several highly regarded foundations. A minority of the group, which included medical and nonmedical members, favored sweeping reform—a national health care system with government regulations to coordinate all patient care. Others disagreed about the need for universal coverage and the amount of government regulation. The Depression and World War II interrupted the debate.

As Truman promoted his bill, the AMA opposed it, saying that it was "socialized medicine" and would interfere with doctor-patient relationships and quality of care. By this time, private insurance provided many voluntary and commercial insurance plans for hospital care, so those Americans who could afford insurance were covered. There was limited support for Truman's national health insurance bill, and Congress defeated it.

Truman then appointed a panel to suggest other reforms. The President's Commission on the Health Needs of the Nation (Magnuson Commission) suggested that the government fund research. One result was the National Institutes of Health, established at Bethesda, Maryland. The government also funded some medical schools and established more scholarships and loans to ease the growing shortage of nurses.

By the 1960s, many Americans were confident that they received the finest, most up-to-date health care in the world. About half had insurance to cover at least some hospital and doctor bills, and access to care was better than ever before. Yet many problems remained, especially for the rural and urban poor and aging Americans.

The Search for Solutions: 1963 to the Present

When Lyndon B. Johnson became president in 1963, he faced enormous challenges. The voice of the black civil rights movement was heard across America, and public attention was focused on the many problems minorities faced, including poverty, unemployment, and inferior education and health care. Americans of other races, many of them children, likewise suffered from inadequate health care. A growing number of people were living longer, and many were spending their last years in poverty, despite Social Security benefits.

Around the country, people showed increasing compassion toward the poor and looked toward government to allay these problems. Johnson instituted a massive program of reforms he called the Great Society. Declaring "war on poverty," he said:

> *Many Americans live on the outskirts of hope, some because of their poverty and some because of their color, and all too many because*

of both. Our task is to help reduce their despair with opportunity. And this administration today, here and now, declares unconditional war on poverty in America.[1]

Help for the Poor and Elderly. By the 1960s, about 70 percent of Americans had private health insurance, while 30 percent did not. About 60 percent of people in poverty lacked health insurance.

Health care for a poor family could be tedious and far-flung: A mother would take her infant to a well-baby clinic for checkups, while getting free immunizations at the local health department. Suppose the baby got sick? In that case, she might go to the emergency room of the community hospital. The adults in the family might receive care for a chronic condition such as diabetes at the outpatient clinic sponsored by the university medical school in their area. Older children might be seen by the school nurse, then referred to another clinic or hospital for needed care. All this took time, effort, and transportation as people traveled to various places, often waiting a long time to see a doctor. With no primary care practitioner to oversee the process, poor families ended up with fragmented care in various facilities and little follow up.

Furthermore, statistics showed that the poor and minorities—blacks, Native Americans, and Hispanics—had higher rates of illness, more days lost from work, a greater infant mortality rate, and a shorter life expectancy. Most poor children had not seen a doctor by age four and about 25 percent had significant health problems. One study of poor families in Ohio showed that only 8 percent of the children had received the standard childhood immunizations.[2] Clearly, the health care sys-

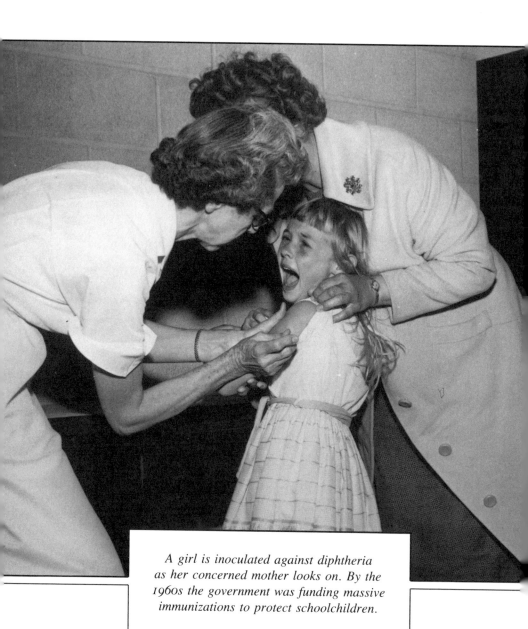

A girl is inoculated against diphtheria as her concerned mother looks on. By the 1960s the government was funding massive immunizations to protect schoolchildren.

tem left millions unserved or underserved. Among those urging reform were physicians, nurses, and other health care workers who cared about the disadvantaged.

After Truman's attempt to pass national health insurance legislation failed, later presidents, including John F. Kennedy, said the government should at least sponsor health plans for the indigent (poor) and people over age sixty-five. The 1960s were a time of economic growth and a low federal deficit, which helped these new government expenditures gain public and political support.

The Medicare program was launched in 1965. At that time, nearly one third of the nation's elderly lived below the poverty line. Middle-class elderly people were being impoverished by the cost of hospitalization or chronic illness. In many cases, their children suffered financially to help pay their bills. Medicare contained two major components: Part A was mandatory and covered hospitalization and acute care funded with payroll deductions and contributions from employers; Part B was an optional plan to pay doctors' fees and nonhospital-related expenses, funded through general revenues and monthly premiums (at that time, a few dollars) paid by the insured elderly.

To finance health care for the poor, Congress approved the Medicaid program, which began in 1967. It involved a combination of state and federal funds to reimburse physicians, hospitals, and other care providers for specific services and supplies. People who qualified for Medicaid could choose among private services as well as public clinics and university outpatient departments. Medicaid gave millions of people more access to care, although many physicians and providers chose not to accept Medicaid patients. States administered their own Medicaid programs and most set fees lower than those collected from private insurance. As costs grew through the years, doctors and clinics in very poor rural and urban areas were hard-pressed to make ends meet on Medicaid fees alone.

Addressing Other Problems. By the 1960s, the hospital shortage was no longer a serious problem, but the lack of overall planning had resulted in certain imbalances—not enough beds for acute care, for example, and surpluses of obstetrical beds. A woman who went to the hospital to deliver a baby might have her choice of rooms while a postoperative patient had to wait for a bed in the surgical unit of the hospital. Duplication of facilities and services in the same locale was common. While this made care more convenient for many people, it also increased costs as hospitals raised fees to pay for equipment and to maintain larger staffs.

    States set up commissions to study these kinds of problems. These groups recommended comprehensive joint planning by state and local authorities in order to avoid wasting taxes and other resources. As nonprofit institutions, hospitals were not geared to think in terms of cost-effectiveness as profit-driven businesses do. They seldom used the methods of cost accounting or forecasting that other businesses use to predict needs, costs, and profits.

    Another concern was the persistent shortage of nurses and the scarcity of women and minority physicians. Financial aid and educational support was made available to more minority students. Medical colleges enrolled more women and minorities, who, it was hoped, would later practice in disadvantaged communities.

    The number of physicians increased by 50 percent between the mid-1960s and the 1980s. However, most chose to become specialists, and the distribution was such that many towns and regions still had no doctors. To bring doctors to these areas, the federal government created the National Health Service Corps in 1971. It awarded scholarships and stipends for living expenses to medical students, who were required to give a year of service in rural clinics or inner city health centers for every year of aid they had received. Over the next twelve years, the corps would place more than 13,000 doctors. Unfortunately, a 1992 study showed that only about 10 percent stayed in these areas after fulfilling their service obligation.[3] To raise the number of primary care doctors, the 1971 Health Manpower Act also gave direct funds to train physicians in family care practice.

Other government grants were made available to nursing students, especially those seeking advanced degrees in special areas of need, such as psychiatric nursing or public health. Yet the shortage of nurses persisted. Nurses were poorly paid compared to many other professionals, even though a four-year college degree had replaced three-year hospital training schools as the main route to this career. They worked shifts around the clock and often were burdened with too many patients and other duties. Once, nursing and teaching had been among the few careers approved for women; but after the 1960s, women had more options in fields such as law, medicine, and business. Many chose professions that offered higher wages and more prestige.

In response, the 1976 Health Professions Educational Assistance Act aimed to ease the nursing shortage as well as supply more doctors and nurses for underserved regions. This act did lead to greater numbers of professionals, including more nurses in regions and specialties that had the greatest need. Still, many professionals did not choose to work in underserved regions or, if they did, they often left those areas after a few years.

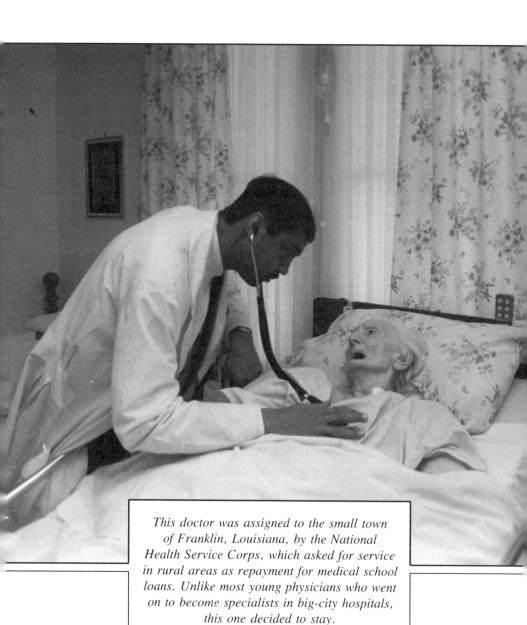

This doctor was assigned to the small town of Franklin, Louisiana, by the National Health Service Corps, which asked for service in rural areas as repayment for medical school loans. Unlike most young physicians who went on to become specialists in big-city hospitals, this one decided to stay.

More Government Funding. Besides setting up national insurance for the needy and elderly and funding professional grants, the government built new community health centers as a solution to fragmented, inaccessible health care. The centers were located in urban and rural areas, and services were designed to meet the needs of the population. By the 1980s about eight hundred such centers existed, serving about 4.2 million people.[4]

During the 1970s, government grants and state monies also funded numerous community mental health centers throughout the nation. Mental health care had come a long way from the days when people were hidden at home, left to wander the streets, or sent to institutions for long-term custodial care. By the 1940s, the military had added psychiatric services, and scientists wrote about the many environmental and social influences on mental health. In 1946 Congress established the National Institute of Mental Health as part of the National Mental Health Act, which channeled federal money into direct treatment, training, and research.

After the 1950s, effective drugs became available for such conditions as depression, mania, and schizophrenia. New research showed the value of certain psychotherapies in treating patients. State hospitals still did most inpatient treatment, but new, privately run psychiatric facilities joined them.

In 1963 President Kennedy delivered the first presidential message on mental health to Congress. With Kennedy's support, Congress passed the Mental Retardation Facilities and Community Mental Health Construction Act. Funding was allocated to community mental health centers that offered counseling, emergency care, educational programs, consultation to teachers, police, and others in the community, and referrals to different social services.

In 1977 President Jimmy Carter renewed support for this branch of health care and appointed a President's Commission on Mental Health. The commission recommended more collaboration between hospitals and the community and follow-up care for those with chronic mental illness. Again, federal money was allotted, for training and for programs to increase public awareness, protect patients' rights, and conduct research into causes and treatments.

Insurance coverage for mental health remained less than that for physical conditions, with about 13 percent of all payments coming from private insurance compared with 28 percent of all general health care costs. Policies usually limited coverage to a certain number of hospital days and set rigid limits on the dollar amount that could go toward mental health care during the insured's lifetime.

Increased Government Control. As the government funded more and more of the nation's health care, it attempted to influence cost and efficiency. By the 1970s, Medicare and Medicaid provided coverage for the aged, poor, disabled, unemployed, blind, those who were unable to work, and dependent children with one parent. The government set rates for reimbursing doctors for specific services.

Yet there was nothing to prevent costs from rising rapidly each year. By 1974 the federal government was paying more than $40 billion a year for health care, compared with $5 billion in 1964. Congress tried to encourage cost containment by passing a comprehensive health planning act that asked communities to set health care priorities and distribute equipment, facilities, and resources in a cost-effective way. Despite the growth of national health care plans around the world, Americans continued to resist this idea. Small, scattered local reforms were the rule.

In another effort to contain costs during the 1970s, Congress also mandated America's physicians to form regional Professional Standards Review Organizations (PSROS) to review the treatment plans and discharge goals for Medicare and Medicaid patients. Efficiency was a major concern. By the 1970s, there were too many hospital beds in many areas, and states began insisting that new hospitals get prior approval. Two government panels studied hospital efficiency, costs, and medical care for the poor, but, according to author Odin Anderson, the "tone in both reports was confusion and frustration."[5] While more federal control was viewed as one solution, the AMA and American Hospital Association (AHA), with powerful lobbyists, opposed it, along with citizens who believed government control should be limited in a free enterprise society. Many said the federal government was in no position to make wise decisions about health care for individuals, states, or communities. Pointing to the inefficiency and waste in other government-run programs, critics said America's health care might deteriorate under federal control.

Other recommendations followed. New government panels advised that health care be better coordinated, preferably through more health maintenance organizations (HMOs) and other group systems (discussed in Chapter Seven). The goal was to foster more competition among caregivers and encourage them to increase their efficiency while reducing prices. Institutions were urged to use more physician assistants and nurse clinicians rather than more costly M.D.s when possible. Hospitals were asked to improve their management procedures and to share services, considering whole geographic regions when deciding what equipment or services to provide. Costs could also be cut by emphasizing preventive care and educating Americans about health and the best ways to use services. Yet the system had always been geared to reward providers for treating illness, not for preventing it.

Spiraling Health Costs. Despite these efforts, costs—especially for hospital care—became a worse problem after the 1970s. As costs rose, outlays from insurance, individuals, and government soared, while the U.S. economy turned sluggish in the face of growing competition from global markets. Other factors—increased rates of violence, a larger, aging population, drug and alcohol abuse, and the AIDS epidemic—further drove up costs. Rising rates of teen pregnancy and more single-parent families headed by poor women resulted in more people using Medicaid funds. As the costs of Medicaid and Medicare grew, so did the national debt. The federal deficit reached an alarming trillion dollar mark during the 1980s.

Private insurance handled by commercial carriers continued to be the main mode of health care payment. These companies collected annual premiums with which they paid hospitals and other caregivers on the fee-for-service basis that had developed during the late 1800s.

But some changes had taken place. More people had begun using the managed care services of HMOs. By 1988 about 18 percent of all private insurance payments went to those organizations. Preferred Provider Organizations (PPOs), groups of physicians and other health care providers, were also negotiating with insurance companies to provide care at a discount. About 11 percent of private insurance payments went to PPOs in 1988.

During Ronald Reagan's presidency (1981–1989), there was a strong push to reduce government activity in general. The administration favored cutting welfare and some other entitlements. Supporters who favored less government control of health care, business, and other areas of life said that this would be good for the economy and encourage individuals to take more responsibility for themselves. People debated whether there was a basic "right" to health care, with many saying there was not.

Yet, the Medicare and Medicaid programs remained in place and the costs of health care and insurance premiums climbed, while business profits and workers' wages seldom kept pace. The number of people living below the poverty line rose during the 1980s, as did unemployment. This had a major impact on health care, since the U.S. system of insurance was tied to the workplace.

Faced with mounting costs, businesses felt the pinch of paying their share, usually 80 percent, of employee health benefits. Large corporations had to pay more when hospitals partially offset unpaid bills by charging higher rates to patients with private insurance. In turn, companies asked workers to pay larger shares of their insurance premiums, frequently reducing employee benefit packages.

Despite a growing call for reform, political leaders who proposed it faced barriers. For example, Congress tried to expand Medicare coverage with its Medicare Catastrophic Act of 1988. The act aimed to increase coverage for catastrophic illness and help needier people to pay for hospital care, doctor's fees, and medicines. Funding was to come from new Medicare premiums and higher taxes on the more affluent elderly. Many elderly people already had private insurance, often called "Medigap," for such illnesses. They did not need more and thought it was unfair for them to pay the whole cost of this program. The American Association of Retired

Persons (AARP) was among the groups who opposed the act, and Congress revoked it. Similarly, bills for universal health coverage were introduced regularly into Congress and defeated.

A Vast, Complex System. By the 1990s, health care had become an enormous multibillion-dollar business that employed about 200 million Americans. It was characterized by large institutions, specialized personnel, high technology, and sophisticated drugs and treatments. Americans used health care services routinely, usually at least once or more each year. One of every six Americans was hospitalized at least once annually. The future promised more advances in such areas as organ transplants and gene therapy that might slow the aging process—advances likely to increase the demand for services and the nation's health care bill.

The system had become so vast and complex that some skeptics wondered if controlling costs and improving overall efficiency was even possible. Yet, without a careful plan, said critics, good health care might become a privilege of the wealthy. To fund health care, businesses and government would pay vast sums that could otherwise be used to reduce the federal deficit and build the U.S. economy.

Before 1993, there was no clear public mandate to revamp health care. By the 1992 presidential election, the concerns of middle-class Americans had made health care a pivotal issue. More citizens spoke out for health care reform. In a September 1993 *New York Times*/CBS poll, 61 percent of those polled answered "yes" when asked: "Would you be willing to pay higher taxes so all Americans have health insurance that they can't lose no matter what?"[6] More than half also said employers should be required to pay most of the health insurance for workers.

According to poll taker Edward H. Lazarus, "Voters want to see action on health care, but they don't know what action they want."[7] People discussed the pros and cons of private systems versus socialized ones run by the government. Polls showed that while Americans wanted guaranteed coverage for everyone, lower costs, and high-quality care, they opposed rationing of care, long waits for doctors and treatments, less choice, and less innovation in technology, new treatments, and drugs.[8] In socialized and government-run health care systems, trade-offs are common—for example, the benefit of universal coverage is balanced against the drawbacks of longer waits for appointments and less access to high technology.

So while asking for change and help from the federal government, people also held high expectations and did not want to give up things they liked about their health care. About 80 percent of Americans said they were satisfied with their present care, although some worried about the future. Those who liked their present situation expressed fears that under a new plan they might end up paying more for less. As the health care debate took shape and people discussed ways to meet the demand for lower costs, universal insurance, access to care, and high quality, it became clear that many thorny issues would need to be resolved.

The High Cost of Health Care: A Closer Look

When Wendy Sommers was twenty-five years old, she found a lump on her leg. At the time, Sommers was part owner of a clothing store in New York City. She did not have health insurance but bought some about a month after she found the lump, even though her doctor had said the lump was benign (noncancerous) and need not be removed. When the lump kept growing, she saw another doctor who advised surgery. The growth turned out to be cancerous.

Shocked and worried, Sommers then found out that her insurance would not pay for treatment because the lump was a preexisting condition—present before she bought her policy. Within a year, cancer was found in her bones. She needed two more operations, including a knee replacement as an alternative to amputation, at a cost of $70,000. Hours of expensive physical therapy followed, coupled with a lack of income from not being able to work much of the time. "Emotionally, I was destroyed," Sommers told author Shirley Streshinsky.[1]

She declared bankruptcy but still could not pay her bills. The cost of health care had taken all the money she had put into her store. A poor credit rating left her unable to qualify for a car loan or to rent an apartment.

Each year, thousands of other Americans have found themselves in a similar situation when illness struck. Health care costs have risen faster than the prices of other goods and services, as reflected by the consumer price index. Individuals and families may be able to afford occasional care but few have the means to cope with major illnesses or long-term care. For that reason, they have relied on insurance coverage. In 1960, Americans paid 56 percent of their own health care costs, but by 1991, that figure had declined to 22 percent.[2] That coverage has become more costly, and for some people, less secure, in recent years.

The Uninsured and Underinsured. As was noted earlier, paying for health care almost always involves a third-party payment insurance plan. The majority of Americans get private medical care from a medical doctor and a community hospital, and the bills are paid, at least in part, by their insurance companies.

As of 1993, 37 million Americans (about 15 percent of the population) had no health insurance. Over a two-year period, far more—about 61 percent of Americans—have been uninsured at some time. They are unemployed, work part-time or at jobs that do not include benefits, or are "uninsurable"—refused insurance, often because they are classified as high-risk applicants. Companies that avoid these people do what critics call "cream-skimming," taking on only people who are unlikely to need expensive care.

Blue Cross and Blue Shield plans have traditionally

These people, part of a massive layoff at Eastern Airlines, are waiting to sign up for unemployment benefits. Along with their jobs, they lost their health insurance; some of them will have trouble receiving coverage again.

accepted open enrollment—new subscribers regardless of health history—and have nearly 80 million subscribers. About 11 million of these are nongroup members with higher than normal risks of needing health care. In most companies, premiums for high-risk people are much higher than for lower-risk people, as the insurance company's costs are higher.

Companies look for new subscribers to offset the costs of higher-risk people. To attract new, low-risk customers, companies may offer them lower rates while raising rates for current subscribers. The company then invites current subscribers to reapply at the new, lower rate, but can refuse to give this cheaper coverage to those with a history of expensive, chronic conditions. This practice, while judged cruel by some people, is seen as necessary by the companies. They compete with other companies for healthier members and must cover their subscribers' bills in order to stay in business. Weeding out sick and high-risk people is a way to stay competitive.

One example of these practices, which some analysts call "policy churning," is a California family of four described by *New York Times* reporter Gina Kolata. Mother Kathleen Renshaw said their premiums soared to $16,000 a year within five years after her daughter was found to have only one kidney—and it was damaged. Although the family belonged to a large group health plan, their rate was doubled each year (the maximum increase allowed by California law) until they could no longer afford it. No other insurance carrier would accept them.[3]

The number of uninsured Americans grew about 50 percent between 1977 and 1993, at which time it included about 12 million children under age eighteen, as well as many elderly, working poor, and mentally ill persons.[4] About half a million American women were not covered for pregnancy. According to Raymond Wheeler, "Most of these people live constantly at the brink of medical disaster, hoping that the symptoms they have or the pain they feel will prove transient or can somehow be survived, for they know that no help is available to them."[5]

During the early 1990s, one fifth of all young adults from age eighteen to age twenty-four also had no insurance. Simple coverage for healthy, single people in their twenties cost from $1,200 to $2,400 a year. Some people rationalize, "I'm young and healthy and I take care of myself, so I won't buy insurance—I can use that money for other things." But others foot the bill for the uninsured, as hospitals pass unpaid costs along to patients with private insurance (called "cost-shifting").

Sometimes, people find they are underinsured. Douglas Symes of San Francisco was in this predicament after accidentally cutting off his left hand while using a power saw to do home improvements. A neighbor rushed him to a hospital where a skilled microsurgeon was able to reattach his hand and save it, except for one finger. His bills totaled about $60,000, but he had insurance—a low-cost policy with a high deductible because of his past excellent health.

After surgery, Symes worked hard to get his insurance company to pay the part he believed they owed. He made numerous phone calls and wrote letters. One stumbling block was that the hospital where he had received treatment did not belong to the group that had contracted with his insurance company. Yet his case had been an emergency. His surgeon verified that it would have been dangerous to move him after microsurgery. After nearly a year, the company paid the surgeon and most of the hospital bill. But it balked at paying the

$1,000 a month for physical therapy that Symes needed to get back use of the muscles and joints in his hand, important for his photography career. His coverage had turned out to be inadequate for the cost of a serious health problem.[6]

Losing Coverage. Worries over health care costs influence many decisions and lead to "job-lock," where people stay in jobs they want to leave to avoid losing their insurance. A 1992 *New York Times*/CBS poll found that 36 percent of people living in households with incomes between $15,000 and $29,999 said they or a member of their household had stayed in a job they wished to leave solely because of health insurance.

People can lose their insurance after a job change or when insurance companies cancel high-risk people. According to a 1987 survey of two thousand insurance policies, about 57 percent did not cover preexisting conditions, among them heart disease, cancer, AIDS, alcoholism, brittle bones, depression, juvenile onset diabetes, drug addiction, epilepsy, cerebral palsy, multiple sclerosis, chronic hepatitis, hemophilia, lupus erythematosus, schizophrenia, wheelchair dependency, or Raynaud's disease. Some policies offer coverage but exclude many various conditions, including AIDS, drug addiction, breast tumors, bursitis requiring surgery, chronic recurring cystitis, fractured spinal discs, herpes simplex, migraine headaches, heart abnormality, carpal tunnel syndrome, and ulcerative colitis. Some companies also refuse people who work in what they call high-risk places: car washes, hospitals, convenience stores, doctors' offices, nursing homes, and parking lots.

Despite taking measures to reduce costs, insurance companies steadily raised their premiums from the 1970s to 1994. The costs have risen as much as 50 percent a year, with some employers paying out as much as 30 percent of total salaries to insure their employees.[7] Dr. Denman Scott, a senior vice president of the American College of Physicians, said, "The system that exists now is ridiculous."[8] He especially criticized the way in which private insurance carriers refuse high-risk applicants, who must then rely on public providers that legally have to accept anyone.

Worthless Insurance. Faced with rising costs and trouble finding a company that would accept them, some people relied upon newer, lesser-known companies. Unfortunately, some of these companies have turned out to be dishonest while others have failed due to mismanagement. The General Accounting Office estimated that between January 1988 and June 1991, more than 400,000 people, often employees of small businesses or unemployed people seeking cheaper group plans, were the victims of suspicious insurance plans. Many victims were well-educated professionals. As the claims came in, the failing companies lacked the money to pay them.

California resident Camille Ewing faced such a situation after having heart transplant surgery that cost $200,000. The hospital sued the family, and they had to sell their home. "We're in the process of losing everything," Mrs. Ewing told *New York Times* reporter Barry Meier.[9] Not only were the Ewings left with huge unpaid bills, they joined the ranks of those who have developed serious illnesses while on one plan, then have to apply for new insurance on the basis of such a preexisting condition.

Mrs. Ewing called their experience "a nightmare. You didn't know where things began or ended."[10] She dealt with numerous agents, brokers, billing agencies and claims administrators. While this was going on, the

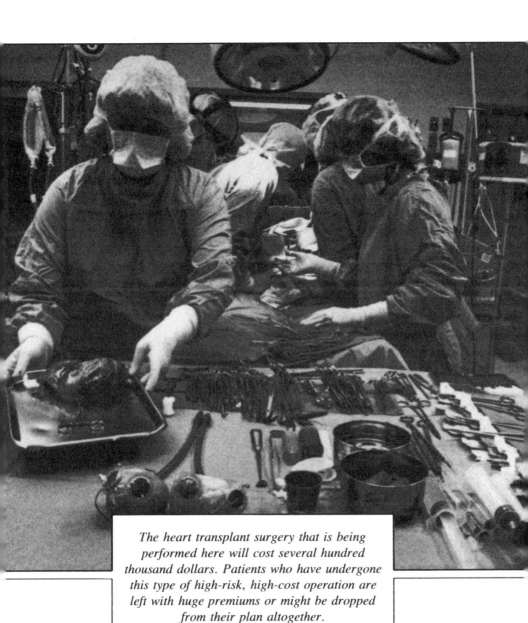

The heart transplant surgery that is being performed here will cost several hundred thousand dollars. Patients who have undergone this type of high-risk, high-cost operation are left with huge premiums or might be dropped from their plan altogether.

Ewings were still paying their $700-a-month premium to guarantee they could not be dropped if the insurance company was able to reorganize or become part of another company.

During the 1980s, the U.S. Department of Justice set up a new unit to investigate insurance fraud. Some states enacted new laws to protect people, as well as warning insurance agents that they may be held liable if they sell worthless plans. States also began regulating multiple-employer insurance trusts and have passed laws that would keep unlicensed providers from operating in their states. In the meantime, the issues of cost and reliability of insurance became a central part of the health care debate.

Behind Soaring Costs. Many reasons for the high cost of health care were discussed earlier as they relate to the way the American system developed throughout history. New public entitlements without cost controls during the 1960s contributed to these costs, which, by 1994, were increasing almost three times faster than the rate of inflation. Lack of overall planning, increasing demand for new technology and treatments, and the fee-for-service method of payment were other factors.

Of all money spent on health care in 1992, about 42 percent went to hospitals, 19 percent to physicians, 6 percent for dental care, 7 percent for drugs, 8 percent for nursing home care, and the remainder to a wide variety of services, including research and preventive care. The United States spent 38 percent more than Canada, 88 percent more than Germany, and 124 percent more than Japan, yet those nations provided coverage for all citizens.

A look back in history shows a steep rise in overall health care costs. Costs rose an average annual rate of

10.4 percent from 1950 to 1985 and an average of nearly 13 percent per year between 1970 and 1987 to an annual rate of 14 percent in 1993. Between 1950 and 1993, national health care expenditures (paid by individuals, corporations, and government) rose from $12.7 billion to $940 billion. Rates rose dramatically each year during the early 1990s, from $660 billion in 1990 (about $2,600 for each person) to $736 billion in 1991 to $839 billion in 1992 to $940 billion in 1993.

General inflation accounted for about 32 percent of the annual rise, while inflation associated just with health care and products (wage increases, equipment, expansion) made up 22 percent. Population growth, the use of new technology, and an increase in the services provided to all patients contributed about 35 percent to these yearly increases.

More Usage by More People. Since the 1970s, more Americans, including the growing numbers of poor and elderly, used more health care services, including expensive new technology and prescription drugs. During that same period, the government spent more than $2 billion a year on medical research. That sum continued to rise as new health problems such as AIDS emerged, and the public clamored for treatments and cures.

A sharp rise in both the usage and the unit cost of care (price for a given service) took place after Congress funded Medicare and Medicaid. These programs increased spending by eventually covering inpatient and outpatient hospital care, lab and X-ray services, physician and nursing services, and home health services. The Social Security Act of 1972 added family planning and certain dental services, prescriptions, and eyeglasses. Health care analyst Eli Ginzberg said that, as a result, "hospitals acquired new equipment, added wages, established a weaker defense against the wage and salary demands of their allied health and service workers, and otherwise increased their outlays substantially. They did all this knowing full well that their expenses would be reimbursed by third-party payers; that is, by insurance companies or the government."[11]

Third-party payment, whether by private insurance or the government, has been blamed for rising costs. Critics say this system insulates most Americans from the true cost of the services they use and encourages people to try any service they think might help them, even going to the doctor for a common cold. When someone else is paying, consumers are less motivated to shop around or compare prices and services. As patients pay less, there is more demand for more services and for a higher quality and level of care. Higher demand drives costs even higher.

Do patients who receive cheaper health care have lower costs in the long run because they get help earlier and thus prevent more severe and expensive problems? In the Rand Corporation's Health Insurance Experiment (1974 to 1982), the opposite happened: A group of people who had free care used services so often that their total costs were 50 percent higher than those of the group whose plans required them to pay up to 95 percent of the costs. Interestingly, the study found that health status was not affected by this reduced use of care, with two exceptions: people with high blood pressure (which increased slightly during the study) and people with very low incomes.[12] Factors related to poverty, such as inadequate nutrition, probably played a role in this outcome.

Hospital Costs. The cost of hospitalization has risen fastest of all. Among the many costs borne by hospitals are employee salaries (often for twenty-four-hour coverage a day), operating and treatment rooms, emergency rooms, intensive care, drugs, labs, supplies (about 45 percent of hospital budgets), anesthetics, record keeping, and technology. As knowledge continues to expand, hospitals run more training programs for their staffs, another expense. Of all institutional care, long-term care costs the most. As the aged population has increased, long-term care has taken an ever larger share of the health costs paid by individuals.

After the Fair Labor Standards Act was applied to hospitals in 1966, costs increased even more. It requires that when wages for lower-paid workers are increased, other people must get more, too, in order to maintain the same differential in their wages.

Other factors have driven up hospital costs. Philanthropy and government grants have declined since the 1970s. Many hospitals have had to borrow money, which means they are saddled with debts. As hospitals compete for paying patients, administrators are pressed to provide better services, food, and equipment than other hospitals in the area. Unlike citizens in many other nations, Americans seldom have to travel long distances to use the newest equipment, since so many hospitals own the same technology.

Many Americans do not examine their hospital bills. Those who do often cannot understand the complicated charges and codes on the bills. The fees charged to patients may not reflect the actual cost of a service or an item. Itemized hospital bills may show startling figures, such as $50.00 for water and $10.00 for cotton balls. These charges reflect the mix of paying and nonpaying patients that hospitals serve and the fact that insurance companies often pay less than the total bill. Bills may also contain errors. In 1993 the General Accounting Office estimated that 99 percent of all hospital bills contained overcharges.[13] In a study by an insurance group, the average hospital bill contained nearly $1,400 in extra charges.[14]

Physician Fees. In the early 1990s, physician fees accounted for about 20 percent of all health care expenditures. Physicians also have a great impact on the use of hospitals, medication, lab tests, and various services. Independent physicians decide what to charge for certain procedures or amounts of time, usually similar to what other physicians in the region charge, then bill the patient or insurance company. When insurers pay only part of the bill, patients are expected to pay the rest. Medicare has adopted a system based on the prevailing rate, which takes into account the fees charged in a given community. Medicare reimburses a doctor up to 75 percent of this rate.

Health care reformers have said that a shortage of primary care physicians (those in general practice, internal medicine, and pediatrics) increases costs. When primary care doctors see patients first, they may save health care dollars by treating problems themselves and recommending specialists and other procedures only if they seem needed. When numerous people see only part of a patient's problems, they may take longer to diagnose and treat it.

Yet in America, since the early 1900s, more doctors have become specialists. The number of medical students choosing primary care went from 37 percent in 1982 to about 14.6 percent in 1992.[15] "We should try to achieve a 50-50 balance," says Dr. Robert Harmon, administrator of the U.S. Health Resources and Services Administration.[16] In Great Britain, the government has created a system with about equal numbers of general practitioners and specialists.

One reason many physicians choose to specialize is that each field of medicine involves so much knowledge. Many prefer to gain in-depth knowledge in one area, rather than try to keep up with a number of them. Also, generalists earn far less than specialists, such as surgeons or radiologists. For example, a primary care doctor may spend an hour examining a patient with abdominal pain, then take additional time reviewing lab test results before diagnosing the problem as gallstones. The fee for these services might range from $50 to $90. The surgeon who removes the patient's gallbladder spends perhaps three hours preparing for and performing the operation and another few hours on postoperative check-ups and record keeping, for a fee ranging from $1,200 to over $3,000.

Because medical training takes many years, physicians may not start their professional practice until they are about thirty years old. They may finish medical school with debts ranging from $5,000 to $100,000, with most owing more than $30,000.[17] The costs of opening an office can be more than $100,000 and running a practice—rent, supplies, equipment, and staff for the office as well as extra costs, such as malpractice insurance—is high. This encourages many doctors to choose higher-paying specialties.

For their part, physicians have faced record numbers of malpractice cases, in which patients sue doctors, hospitals, and others for negligence. In some cases, juries have awarded patients millions of dollars in damages. Cases can involve inappropriate medication or carelessness, but in some instances, such as birth defects or injuries, the cause of the problem is unclear. Even when physicians are sure they are not at fault, insurance companies often choose to pay a sum of money to settle the suit and avoid an expensive court battle. The fact that attorneys who take these cases may collect up to half of the money awarded has also been denounced by critics of the current system.

As a result of more litigation, malpractice insurance has become more costly. By the 1970s, some surgeons were paying annual premiums of up to $20,000. Between 1974 and 1975 malpractice rates for physicians and hospitals doubled and tripled, then slowed down to rise about 20 percent a year. These costs have been passed on to patients in the form of higher fees. Insurance companies, faced with higher medical bills, have also raised their premiums, which means higher charges for consumers.

The threat of lawsuits can also influence physicians to order more tests and do extra record keeping to protect themselves. Some physicians say that fear of lawsuits spurs them to use more "textbook medicine." Says a forty-nine-year-old cardiologist practicing in Connecticut, "I do everything by the book and order tests to be sure I'm covered." The cost of such "defensive medicine" has been estimated at $25 billion a year.[18]

Malpractice claims declined somewhat during the late 1980s, and some analysts claim they are not a valid reason for rising health care costs. But malpractice premiums remain high for obstetricians, surgeons, and anesthesiologists. A 1990 survey by *Medical Economics* magazine found that these premiums were, on average, about 3.7 of all physicians' practice receipts. The U.S. Department of Health and Human Services stated that the total cost of malpractice was less than 1 percent of total health care spending.[19] In looking for ways to save health care dollars, some plans have included malpractice reforms that would limit the amount patients could collect in court for "pain and suffering." Others have proposed limiting the fees collected by attorneys.

Cost of Procedures. Medical procedures, especially diagnostic tests and treatments using expensive technology, add greatly to health costs. As new technology has come along, it has been made available, with no sustained effort to evaluate cost-effectiveness. Again, patients have been eager to take advantage of whatever might help them. Doctors, wanting to help their patients and avoid being labeled negligent, have often utilized this technology.

Two devices—CAT (computerized axial tomography) scanners and MRI (magnetic resonance imaging) machines—enable physicians to visualize deep areas of the brain, spine, and other places in the body without surgery. By the late 1980s, they cost more than 1.5 million dollars each, up from $600,000 in the 1970s. Operating costs were more than $200,000 a year. The number of CAT scans done each year has risen, too: from 300,000 scans to 1.5 million between 1980 and 1991.[20]

New discoveries have increased the life spans of people who would have died from their conditions as recently as twenty years ago. Modern technology has thus created ethical dilemmas, because while lifesaving technology may prolong life by a few days, weeks, or months, a patient may remain in a coma with virtually no chance of recovery, at a cost of thousands of dollars a week.

Some physicians are accused of overusing technology and of doing unnecessary surgery. Among the operations viewed as too frequent are Cesarean sections (surgical delivery of babies), which accounted for one fourth of all U.S. births during the early 1990s. Physicians may do C-sections to avert the chance of a problem during childbirth, both for the patients' benefit and to avoid lawsuits, which are high in this area of medi-

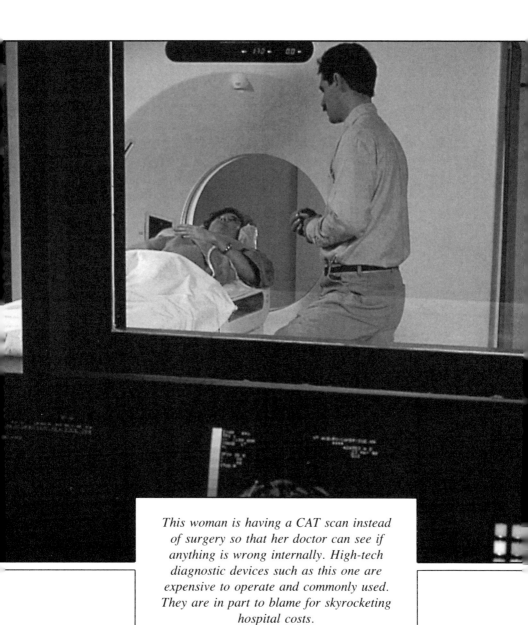

This woman is having a CAT scan instead of surgery so that her doctor can see if anything is wrong internally. High-tech diagnostic devices such as this one are expensive to operate and commonly used. They are in part to blame for skyrocketing hospital costs.

cine. Other types of surgery, including back operations, have been cited as too frequent and often ineffective. Critics complain that surgeries are often performed even when the potential benefit is small. Between 1970 and 1991, the number of cardiac bypass operations rose from 14,000 to 407,000. Many patients are older people who might not benefit much from the procedure.[21] Lifesaving surgeries can be costly (for example, $300,000 for a liver transplant and follow-up care).

Studies have noted that the number of certain surgeries often varies from region to region, although not because of patient differences. Dr. John Wennberg found that people in one Vermont town were seven times more likely to have had a tonsillectomy by age fifteen than people living in a town only a few miles away. The rate of heart surgery was twice as high per capita in Des Moines, Iowa, than in nearby Iowa City.[22] Such variations may occur because there are more physicians practicing in a given area or because doctors in a given place adopt a consistent approach to certain kinds of health problems. This can result in a community "standard of practice" against which doctors' decisions are evaluated.

Analysts think the cost of unnecessary surgery may run as high as $50 billion each year.[23] The total cost of these procedures and services has been estimated at $130 billion a year.[24] This would be about 20 percent of all care. Unnecessary hospital days, also estimated at between 20 and 53 percent of the total days, are linked to this problem.

Paying for Medications. Like other health care services, medications can carry high price tags. The pharmaceutical industry has been criticized for the costs of many prescription drugs. After having a heart transplant operation, people may need medication costing as much as $1,500 a month. Interferon, a drug used to fight cancer, costs several thousand dollars per treatment.

To help offset the costs of research and ensure profits, drug companies have an exclusive legal right to sell the products they create for the next ten years at the price they choose. Sam Peltzman, an economics professor at the University of Chicago, described the situation: "These companies are not charities—they are charging what the market will allow them to charge." The companies are responsible for pleasing shareholders and raising funds for new research and thus "try to maximize their profits," as Peltzman says.[25]

Drug companies contend that drugs, although costly, may save money in the long run. A drug for premature babies' lungs costs hundreds of dollars but can keep infants out of neonatal intensive care units. Drugs for the mentally ill or aged may allow them to live at home rather than in institutions. The prices of developing each individual drug also reflect the costs of research and development. Peltzman says that in the drug industry, "nine out of ten products fail."[26]

A new drug named tacrine became the subject of debate in 1993. It was the first drug to show some effectiveness in treating people with Alzheimers', a devastating chronic brain disease. Tacrine results in slight or no benefit in relieving memory loss for most patients. If past history is any guide, most, if not all, Alzheimers' patients will insist on trying this drug, which costs about $3.50 per person a day in 1993. If only 10 percent of all patients (400,000 people) took it, the annual cost would be more than $500 million, yet only about 80,000 of them would benefit from the drug. The cost per person would be more than $6,000 a year. Reformers ask: Should limits be placed on the use of drugs or on surgeries, tests, and treatments? Who should make such decisions?

Another condition that entails costly drugs is AIDS. Millions of Americans have HIV (human immunodeficiency virus) or full-blown AIDS, and the number has risen steadily since the 1980s. The cost of treating people with HIV and AIDS is presently about $102,000 over each patient's lifetime, up from $85,333 in 1991, according to U.S. Public Health Service statistics.[27]

Fraud, Waste, and Abuse. Critics of the current system say that waste, abuse, and fraud—for example, billing for services not performed or feigning poverty in order to qualify for Medicaid—may account for nearly $200 billion of health care costs, a sizable portion of the total.[28] Waste and abuse include unnecessary tests and procedures as well as the use of procedures with little potential value.

Administrative inefficiency is included in this area. The time and paperwork involved in administering health care and insurance payments is enormous, costing billions of dollars a year—about twenty cents of every health care dollar. Medicare entails special costs because some payments come from the federal government, some from insurance, and some from the patient. When a Medicare patient is hospitalized, up to twenty-six forms need to be filled out. There is a great deal of duplication in paperwork, too.

Paperwork can be so time-consuming that physicians hire full-time employees who do nothing but process forms. Professionals complain that their own paperwork consumes hours a day, time they could spend with patients. A pediatrician in Washington, D.C., said that she and her partner spent twenty-five hours a week processing forms: "The duplication of documentation,

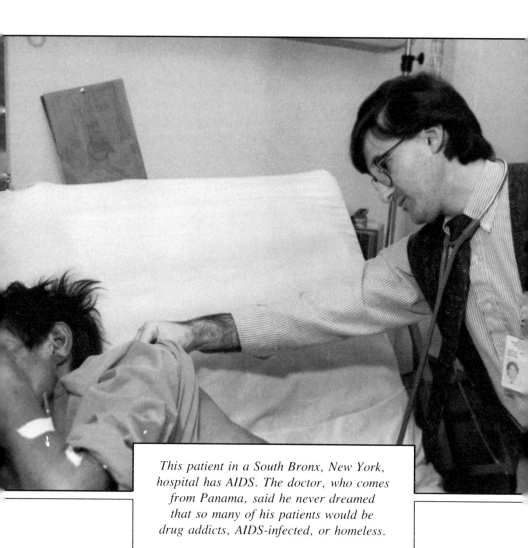

This patient in a South Bronx, New York, hospital has AIDS. The doctor, who comes from Panama, said he never dreamed that so many of his patients would be drug addicts, AIDS-infected, or homeless.

the authorization forms, the insurance claim forms, and all of the complicated and often contradictory instructions as devised by the more than 50 insurance plans we accept are all overwhelming."[29] Dr. Albert Beasley, a Connecticut physician, believes such bureaucratic chores deter talented people from entering the medical profession.[30]

The task of controlling the high cost of health care is a formidable one at the center of every plan for reform. But can costs be cut or even contained while meeting the other major goals of reform as defined by the majority of Americans—namely, that all citizens should have access to quality care throughout their lifetime? And what benefits should such universal care include? The issues of access to care and the quality and quantity of this care are also central to America's health care debate.

Access and Quality

A woman named Elizabeth Glaser took the podium during the 1992 Democratic National Convention. She had contracted AIDS in 1981 through a blood transfusion she received while in the hospital giving birth. As a result, her daughter Ariel and her son Jake, born later, also were infected with the disease, and Ariel had died. Mrs. Glaser was receiving treatment and had become active in helping others, especially children, who were suffering from AIDS.

"Do you know how much AIDS costs?" she asked the audience at the convention. "Over $40,000 a year. Someone without insurance can't afford this. . . . This is not the America I was raised to be proud of, where rich people get care and drugs that poor people can't afford."[1]

Cable News Network correspondent James Rosenthal said that Glaser's speech "made plain to millions watching on television what people across this country are beginning to claim as a new and inalienable birthright: affordable, quality health care for all."[2]

At the 1992 Democratic National Convention, Elizabeth Glaser told a heartrending tale of having contracted AIDS through a blood transfusion when giving birth. She voiced many Americans' anger at a health care system that is inaccessible to the poor.

Access to health care involves issues of cost, as well as the availability of appropriate health care resources in a given area. People also need enough knowledge to choose the best people and places to go to for care and to judge and influence the quality of that care. Whether or not every American has a right to health care has been a long-standing debate.

Health Care—A Right? Is health care a basic right that should be guaranteed to all citizens? This idea has been debated in many societies for years. Central to this debate is the fact that health problems are an individual misfortune, rarely caused by anyone else. Such problems were traditionally viewed as fate or the result of bad luck. Thus, when strangers helped those who were sick, injured, or disabled, they did so out of a sense of compassion or morality, not because they owed these persons help.

If health care is a right, then those who need help get to use the resources of other people—their time, money, skills. Opponents of free health care argue that this limits others' rights in the process. Author Thomas J. Bole III says, "The difficulty is that rights to have one's needs met or one's goods realized, positive rights, usually involve claims on the labors and resources of others. Positive rights circumscribe negative rights, the right to be left alone."[3] Bole points out that positive rights are thus harder to defend than negative ones (leaving people alone) because they impose duties on others, usually strangers, one reason for the persistent opposition to more public funding for welfare and health programs.[4]

Supporters of universal access to health care argue that every person has an equal moral worth and deserves a chance for equal well-being, because health is basic to equal opportunity. They contend that health care is at least as necessary as enough food, clothing, shelter, and education if people are to have a decent standard of living and a chance to succeed.

Going beyond the issue of rights, some reformers argue that not providing a minimum level of health care to all citizens has negative consequences for America as a whole. A population that is not healthy cannot be as productive or reach its potential. In today's increasingly competitive world, human resources are valuable assets, so the whole nation stands to gain if all reach optimum health. And people who need care but lack insurance do receive that care anyway, but at taxpayers' expense. They often resort to more expensive emergency rooms, with more severe problems, because they waited so long to get help.

Despite the controversy over rights and responsibilities, nearly all representative democracies have decided, on moral and practical grounds, to provide universal access to health care. Canada, Japan, Great Britain, and other nations spend a much smaller portion of their national budget on health care than the United States does; they can devote more of their resources to education, transportation, and developing industry, among other things.

Things have been different in America. In colonial times, individual communities assumed some duty to help those perceived as helpless or unable to work and support themselves. Religious groups or town government arranged for the indigent to receive basic food, clothing, and other needs and access to public shelters and hospitals. As the population increased and social problems grew more numerous and complex, the federal government took on a larger role. But there has been no comprehensive national health plan.

Now as health care costs alarm Americans, the middle class speaks out for a "right to health care." Such diverse groups as business leaders, the insurance industry, bipartisan members of Congress, the Consumer's Union, the American Medical Association, the Children's Defense Fund, the American Federation of Teachers, and the American Association for Retired Persons agree that every citizen should have access to care.

How Much Care? Many agree that some health coverage should be provided to all citizens but disagree about the scope and nature of the services people should receive. There is no consensus about what constitutes adequate health care, although people might agree that certain lifesaving measures or treatment of acute disease are basic. The American Medical Association speaks of "a comprehensive package of benefits."[5]

President Clinton's Health Care Task Force examined a variety of options while considering basic health benefits. They stated a goal of giving every citizen the same array of benefits that employees of Fortune 500 companies receive through their insurance plans. Among the benefits being debated are preventive care, both medical and dental, for children and adults; mental health counseling and inpatient treatment; home care; hospice care; long-term care for chronic illness and the elderly; and prescription drugs.

People also debated whether a health plan should provide care for drug and alcohol abuse treatment, unwed pregnancy, and AIDS. Critics expressed resentment at possibly being asked to pay more taxes or higher insurance premiums to cover those who make what they consider to be unhealthy lifestyle choices. A thirty-eight-year-old mother and housewife in New England said, "Why should I and my family, who don't drink or smoke and lead as healthy a life as possible, have to pay for people who make bad choices that cause them to have health problems?" Some members of Congress have proposed charging people less for insurance if they do not smoke, for example.

In shaping a new health care system, Americans have had to decide what should constitute a basic benefits package and how such benefits might be phased in over time, in light of the nation's economy. Should the list include cosmetic surgery as well as immunizations for all children? Experimental cancer drugs and treatments? Medications of unproven value? CAT scans for those with chronic headaches as well as those who have had head injuries? And what kind of authorization or approval will be needed, if any, in deciding what can be used in treating individuals?

Standing in the way of universal access to any kind of care are soaring costs, growing demands for services, new technology and drugs, advances in treatments and cures, and the growing population of elderly, including "baby boomers," those born between 1945 and 1961. In some societies with universal health care, services have been rationed—allocated based on severity of need and other factors. This idea clashes with current American practices of doing whatever might help a patient and a distaste for putting a price tag on people's well-being.

Rationing. "Rationing of health care" is a phrase that makes many Americans shudder. Yet rationing already exists, by default rather than conscious decision making. It takes place when resources are limited and as a result of a two-tiered system that treats the poor differently than the nonpoor. Examples of this de facto rationing occur in emergency rooms, where more critically ill people get faster treatment, and in the distribution of organs, when there is a limited supply for a larger number of patients awaiting transplants.

Dr. Howard H. Hiatt gives another example: communities that have limited numbers of dialysis machines, needed by people who have no functioning kidneys. During the 1970s, some communities set up committees to decide who had priority to use the machines. In one case, they had to decide among a twenty-eight-year-old mother of three, a twenty-two-year-old college senior, a sixty-seven-year-old retired person with no dependents, and a forty-five-year-old married dentist. Choices were often based on things other than medical grounds. In later years, when reviews of such decisions were done, analysts found that "men were chosen over women in a ratio of 2 to 1 and the rejects included disproportionate numbers of the old and the mentally ill."[6]

Questions about who will get limited resources are likely to remain—the highest bidder, the youngest, the most prominent, the person with the most dependents, the one with the best political connections? Such choices can be made by government panels that work with formal, publicly known guidelines, or ad hoc decisions can be made on a local level, as they arise. This may be one of the more difficult decisions to be made in health care planning.

In 1992 Oregon developed a plan some called rationing care, but which state officials called prioritization. Some treatments were to be excluded from Medicaid reimbursement, including cosmetic surgery, self-limiting conditions, and treatments of no proven merit. The plan denied aggressive treatment to people with terminal cancer so far advanced that a patient had virtually no chance to survive. Yet the plan approved organ transplants, which are extremely costly, because they have been shown to succeed in saving lives. The plan did not gain approval from the federal government, but a modified version was later approved after the Clinton administration began in 1993. While some praised the idea behind it, critics said it did not address rising costs, just limited access to some services.

The continuing explosion of technology has huge implications for patient care, medical decisions, and what people expect from their health care. People have expressed fears that in a country with universal health coverage, there would be less access to high technology. Critics point to the waiting lists for certain types of surgery, such as heart bypass, in Canada and Great Britain. However, others point out that between 1988 and 1992, Australia, Canada, France, and Israel did more bone-marrow transplants per capita than the United States, probably as a result of cost control efforts that made this procedure more affordable.

A Two-Class System. Reflecting differences in access to quality services are statistics that show disparities between the health of the poor and nonpoor and among racial groups. Infant mortality rates for black Americans are twice as high as for whites. The poor die earlier from cancer and heart disease and other conditions than do wealthier people, and, again, rates are higher for blacks and Hispanics than for whites. Contributing to these statistics are malnutrition, poor housing, illiteracy, and unemployment, as well as higher rates of contagious illness and violence in many poor communities.

The poor tend to use hospital services at higher rates than middle- and upper-income citizens. Often, they cannot afford to see a doctor sooner and they may not receive immunizations or have money for decent food and living conditions. Providing access to primary care and better outpatient services is a key to real improvement in the health of these Americans. Still another barrier must be overcome—that of access to caregivers, especially primary care doctors. As of the 1980s, many physicians did not accept Medicaid patients, whose fees are set about 20 to 25 percent lower than what hospitals and doctors charge privately insured patients. About 6 percent of all physicians treat about one third of all the Medicaid patients, while 20 percent of physicians see none at all.

Many physicians are also frustrated by this two-class system. The number of for-profit hospitals has risen in past decades. They usually refuse patients without money to pay their bills. One North Carolina doctor expressed "disappointment and anger" about what happened to one of his patients who suffered a traumatic head injury in an auto accident. The neurosurgeon at a given hospital had been told by the administrators not to accept uninsured patients. This doctor wrote that "business managers should not have the final say in determining who gets health care because the less fortunate will always suffer."[7]

Dr. Dan Higgins, director of emergency medicine at St. Francis Medical Center in Lynwood, California, has also seen the problems that come from the poor's lack of access. His hospital serves a population that includes 40 percent MediCal, the Medicaid program in California. During the early 1990s, that state's budget was so tight that MediCal reimbursed at a rate of about forty cents on the dollar. Dr. Higgins found that patients, including many working poor, were coming to the emergency room with increasingly severe problems: "You see people coming in with health problems that could have been treated quite easily if they'd gotten help

These children are bundled up indoors because the heat went off in their New Jersey apartment in December, two-and-a-half weeks ago. It is unlikely that children who grow up in such poverty receive adequate health care.

earlier. But they don't have a doctor. Their child has a fever, sometimes for days, but they don't go for help because they need that money for food or to pay the rent. People are really in trouble out there."[8]

As author H. Jack Geiger points out, one can hardly expect equity in a health care system that is "remote, hospital centered, professionally controlled, fragmented, middle-class in its orientation, and unaware of (or unresponsive to) the social, physical, and biological environments in which both urban and rural poor live. A new kind of institution, differently organized, locally based, and focused on primary care, would do better."[9]

Other Barriers to Access. If all Americans are to have access to quality health care, financial considerations are not the only barriers to surmount. The training and distribution of professionals still leaves many areas unserved. A nursing shortage has fluctuated in severity through the years and persisted into the 1990s. In 1988 a federal commission found that this shortage was widespread throughout the nation. Reasons included the AIDS epidemic, the fact that hospital patients have tended to be sicker, and the increased number of nursing homes, where there are more and sicker patients. In 1988 the Secretary's Commission on Nursing of New York found that the shortage sprang from low average salaries and low rates of increases, a low professional image, low retention, and poor working conditions.

Many areas still lack enough physicians. Most physicians are, in effect, independent businesspeople who can choose where they will locate their practices. Cities and wealthy areas consistently have many more doctors than do inner cities and rural areas. For example, in Beverly Hills, California, an exceptionally affluent five-square-mile (13-square-kilometer) city in west Los

Angeles, there is one internist per 566 people. In another part of the city, in the poor section of Compton, there is one internist for every 19,422 people. People in poverty areas may have to travel a long distance to see a doctor or get to a hospital.

Lack of information may also keep Americans from getting quality care. Even those who are near health care services and have the means to pay for them may not have the knowledge and information to use them most effectively. The 85 percent of Americans who do have health insurance have problems evaluating their care or judging what is best to do next.

Quality of Care. People generally agree that quality care is that which promotes a patient's health and satisfies the patient's needs. The AMA Council on Medical Service defined quality care as that "which consistently contributes to improvement of the quality and/or duration of life."[10] Care may range from unacceptable, or poor, to high quality, or optimal.

As far back as the 1860s, Florence Nightingale, the English woman who developed modern nursing as a profession, set up a method of collecting and reporting hospital statistics. In 1900 the highly regarded Massachusetts General Hospital tried to improve on the evaluation process by using a method called "end result analysis" to analyze cases in which treatment was deemed unsuccessful. But opposition led to the abandonment of this method. Other hospitals set up their own kinds of studies. After the 1960s, the federal government began setting standards geared toward eliminating unnecessary procedures. Their goal was to get the best possible results at the lowest cost, thus lowering bills for Medicare and Medicaid.

Most consumers lack the experience or information

to really compare physicians and care options. The more there are, the harder this choice becomes. Also, there has not been much competition in terms of price among individual physicians, so they must stress quality, which consumers find hard to judge. Medicine is often inexact and uncertain. Health care professionals may disagree about the best treatment or approach. Patients may face a wide range of diagnostic and treatment choices when dealing with a particular condition. Individual practitioners differ, as do customs among different regions and cultures.

Some quality evaluation comes from state laws that require hospitals to meet certain criteria before they are accredited. State licensing boards authorize physicians—M.D.s and D.O.s (osteopaths)—and other health care providers, such as physician assistants, nurse practitioners, physical therapists, psychologists, chiropractors, and others to practice legally after they meet certain qualifications and pass required tests. Physicians have set up ways to judge competence among their members, with systems of peer review, board certification in their specialties, and continuing education requirements. Peer review for physicians has focused primarily on the safety of decisions and technical care.

Americans have expressed concern about the impersonality of some health care they receive, especially when they must see a variety of caregivers. Nursing schools have long included interpersonal relations and psychology courses in their curricula, while more medical schools have added courses on these subjects and ethics in response to criticism and malpractice suits. Health care reform may encourage such efforts and establish more ways for patients to get information about quality of care in order to evaluate it. For example, President Clinton's plan suggests an annual "report card" that gives information about different groups of health care providers. It also proposes to establish a basic benefits package so that people can compare the prices different health care organizations charge for this package. Other major proposals include provisions for quality research, performance measures, and the use of electronic data bases to disseminate information.

As people continue trying to define quality—especially in terms of getting optimum results at the lowest costs—they show concern about many aspects of care. Besides the quality of direct care—treatments and other procedures—interpersonal relations between patient and professionals and hospital staffs will be considered, along with the availability of resources, the amenities of various institutions, and the condition of the patient before and after treatment. Planners, managers, and policy makers involved in health care will be looking at the physical, social, and psychological parts of the system, all of which affect those who give and receive care.

Efforts to Control Costs

The history of America's health care system is one of repeated attempts to control costs. There have been proposals to make hospitals more cost-effective and efficient, limits on the fees federal and state governments would pay for Medicaid and Medicare patients, and emphasis on outpatient treatment to cut down on hospitalization. Businesses have negotiated with insurance carriers to cut costs. Health Maintenance Organizations (HMOs) and other organized groups of providers have offered managed care to their subscribers at a fixed price.

However, critics claim that because reforms have been piecemeal, with no fundamental change in the system itself, costs have continued to rise. Maryann O'Sullivan, director of Health Access, a consumer coalition based in California, says, "As quickly as payers patch the system up, the providers find the spaces between the patches."[1] Analyst Edmund Faltermayer gives an example: "Doctors circumvent Medicare fee limits by seeing patients more often or piling on more tests."[2] The current system not only allows costs to rise, it encourages it, say these critics.

As reforms have been proposed and discarded through the years, a key part of the debate has been the role of the government in a democratic society—how much control should it exercise over health care costs and delivery? Although the federal government now pays about 42 percent of the bill for health care, it has not exercised much control over the system. American health care is more decentralized and informal than that of most other nations. This is partly because America is much larger and more diverse than many other nations, with a heterogeneous mix of some 270 million people living in an area of more than 3.6 million square miles (9.4 million square kilometers).

Reform advocates say that it is unrealistic to expect more and better services while paying lower taxes than people in other industrialized nations and insisting that the government not exercise more control. Opponents of cost controls or price freezing claim that free-market forces, the basis of America's economic system, must be allowed to work as they will and thus set prices.

But do current market forces keep health care prices reasonable? Dr. Alan Garber, medical doctor and economist at Stanford University, says "A fair price normally gets set in a market where there are many well-informed buyers and many sellers and no subsidies or taxes or patents to distort it. In health care, none of these conditions exist."[3] H. Jack Geiger calls the idea that "health care is a rational marketplace that will respond to classic market forces" an "economic fiction."[4]

Previous chapters have shown that high costs come from unnecessary care, overpriced care, inefficient de-

livery of care, and the complex administration of the current system. So, in recent years, various cost-cutting efforts have addressed these areas.

Containing Hospital Costs. Because hospital costs have risen most, many efforts have focused on this part of the system, aiming to cut costs through less usage, stays, shorter more cost-accounting procedures, lower rates of employee turnover (now estimated at about 70 percent), and less hospitalization through more preventive and outpatient care. Along those lines, some insurance coverage has been expanded to include routine examinations in the hope of preventing later hospitalization.

Rate setting was a major effort to cut hospital costs. In rate-setting states, incentives have been provided to encourage hospitals to reduce the numbers of days people spend there. The 1983 amendments to the Social Security Act called for a Prospective Payment System to pay for Medicare patients' hospital care. The payment method is based on Diagnostic Related Groups (DRGs) and took effect in 1984.

DRGs are not based on the number of actual days an individual spends in the hospital or the hospital's actual cost, but rather on the patient's diagnosis, such as being admitted for an appendectomy or pneumonia. DRGs vary according to the patient's grouping into one of twenty-three major diagnostic categories (MDCs), which relate to body systems and are divided into forty-seven smaller groups based on a person's age, sex, and other clinical information. (An additional group includes patients whose diagnosis and surgical procedure do not match.) DRGs also reflect whether the hospital is in a rural or urban setting, with adjustments for its wages, teaching status, and amount of service provided to low-income patients. The use of DRGs has been expanded and used by private insurance companies for larger numbers of people.

With this method, hospitals can profit by lowering their costs to an amount less than the fee paid per DRG, and they may be motivated to keep costs in line with other hospitals in their region. Inpatient expenditures declined during the first few years after the DRG system was introduced. Hospital stays were shorter, and total admissions fell by 2.6 percent in 1984. Women who had uncomplicated childbirths were encouraged to leave the hospital one or two days after their deliveries, in contrast to past years when they might stay a week or more. Patients who had less intrusive surgery, such as that performed with lasers, might leave the same day.

Yet costs have still risen sharply, with a single day in the hospital now resulting in a charge of more than $1,000. Critics of the Prospective Payment System using DRGs also say that some patients are discharged too early in an effort to save money. However, as of 1993, no research clearly supported that claim.

In another effort to reduce the length of hospital stays, many hospitals changed the practice of limiting staff on weekends. With complete staffing seven days a week, patients do not have to spend extra weekend days waiting to have procedures done on weekdays. Some hospitals have formed partnerships, called consortiums, in which they share facilities, services, and even staff members so there is less expensive duplication.

Some people have suggested that insurance companies take a closer look at hospital bills before settling claims. "A patient handing a signed insurance claim form to a hospital admitting nurse is handing over a blank check. The hospital fills in the amount," said New York City resident Jacques Liwer. Mr. Liwer took a close look at the hospital bills that came after his wife had a microscopic glass shard removed from her finger: "The cost of the operation, which required an incision less than a quarter-inch in the finger tip under local anesthesia, was $2,200, excluding the physician's fee. In addition, $200 was charged for the removal of stitches."[5] The Liwer's family physician later said he could have removed the glass shard in his office for about $100.

Liwer is among those who think that insurance companies should approve operations beforehand. Some insurance companies do require a second opinion and prior authorization before a patient has elective (nonemergency) surgery. A number of people also say that insurance companies should ask patients to review their bills to check for errors. Regardless of what reforms are implemented, patients could take some responsibility for finding out costs and making sure charges are accurate.

Paying for the Uninsured. One of the persistent problems in any health care system is paying the price for people who cannot afford their own care. The nature of health care is such that people are going to receive it whether they can pay or not, as no humane society deliberately refuses to aid a person they find suffering or at risk of dying when treatment is available. In this sense, health care is obviously different from many other goods and services that people can do without.

Proposed answers to the dilemma have involved one or more of the following solutions: cutting health care costs in general, finding ways to make health insurance available to all, finding new sources to pay for the uninsured (such as through a national insurance program funded through new taxes or other sources of revenue).

Some people have also proposed community rating

legislation that would prohibit insurance from picking and choosing whom to insure. People who oppose this say that young and healthy people would then be charged higher premiums to help pick up some of the costs of older people and others who need care. At present, all taxpayers share this burden, and young, healthy people stand to benefit later on when they need help.

Providing universal health insurance became a top priority in the health care debate of the early 1990s. Some states had already tried to require all employers to cover workers, but federal laws against such plans were a stumbling block in most cases.

Whether Americans' health insurance will continue to be linked to employment, as President Clinton proposed, or separate from employment, as others, including the League of Women Voters, have suggested, remains to be seen.

Cost-Effective Treatments. The cost of high-tech treatments has led to more discussions of both need and cost-effectiveness. Some physicians say that some unneeded tests can be avoided simply by taking a more comprehensive history while talking with patients. Dr. C. Everett Koop, former U.S. Surgeon General, founded an institute at Dartmouth College that sponsors innovative approaches to health care, such as using low-tech alternatives to high-tech procedures. One technique uses a simple nylon probe to check the circulation in the feet of diabetics, who often lose the feeling in their extremities and might not be aware of sores that become infected. Each year, about 50,000 foot and leg amputations are done on diabetics who develop such problems. Using the probe, a caregiver can locate insensitive areas on the foot and prescribe special shoes that relieve pressure on the vulnerable spots.

Another example deals with more difficult choices. There is a diagnostic procedure for checking blood flow that costs far less than a newer procedure. The old test injects dye and is used about 10 million times annually, with a rate of three hundred fatalities a year. The new technique costs $1 billion, far more than the dye technique, but should prevent all fatalities. Dr. Alan Garber, medical doctor and economist at Stanford University, is among those who worry that unless insurers and HMOs are allowed to refuse to pay for certain treatments they view as outrageously priced, then companies "with a unique product can say the sky's the limit, and we can't afford that."[6]

In Canada and Australia, among other nations, manufacturers are told to price their products reasonably or they will not be purchased. Cost effectiveness is sometimes hard to evaluate in these matters, but scrutiny into pricing of drugs and treatments will likely increase in view of rising costs.

Drug Costs. Limited progress has been made in dealing with the high cost of pharmaceuticals. The rise of generic drugs—compounds that go by their chemical names (for example, tetracycline and ibuprofen) rather than a trade name from the manufacturer—has reduced prices somewhat. People can now buy a generic brand of most compounds at a lower cost. Since wholesale prices for drugs differ greatly, sometimes from ten to forty times less than retail prices, consumer awareness is important when considering generic alternatives. Yet physicians sometimes hesitate to prescribe certain generic formulas, saying they cannot predict their effects and side effects as clearly.

People are debating just what the fair price for a drug is. U.S. pharmaceutical companies conduct extensive, expensive research, often with no guarantee of success. Many products entail a long discovery process and animal and human trials. When a new drug is found, the producer owns the patent for the next ten years. Prices are based on manufacturing costs, clinical factors, marketing and distributing costs, the company's expenses, and the potential for profits.

Some patents involve new drugs that are in great demand, for example, the Alzheimer's drug, tacrine. Critics complain that some companies then charge as much as they can get. For that reason, some people propose reducing the number of years on drug patents.

Critics have also suggested a need for federal controls. Dr. Peter Arno, a health economist at Montefiore Medical Center in the Bronx, New York, says that in pricing a new drug, we should compare it to others with a similar function and consider the cost of the drug in other countries. This would be harder, though, with new classes of drugs. The price would also cover the company's cost of development and what Arno calls "a reasonable rate of return."[7] This "cost-plus pricing" method is used in the defense industry. What about the costs of developing unusable drugs? Some say such overhead could be factored in, but that costs could be cut by reducing waste and inefficiency, doing only focused, well-planned research.

The government pays for some drugs through the Medicaid program and has a policy of paying the lowest price at which that drug is available. President Clinton's health care reform team proposed payments for all prescription drugs. As a result, people have debated which drugs will be covered, if any coverage is approved. Will it include contraceptives? What about drugs that control but do not cure disease, for example AZT, used to prolong the lives of AIDS patients, at a cost of about $40,000 a year?

The government may go on to consider how to influence prices or find cheaper ways to buy drugs. Federal drug advisory panels are now prohibited from considering price when they recommend licensing new drugs. Another factor that might influence drug prices is membership in large groups, such as HMOs. Large organizations may negotiate better prices for drugs as they do for other services.

The Growth of Managed Care. One of the biggest changes in the health care system has been the growth of managed care, primarily HMOs. The goal of managed care is to increase competition and efficiency through the establishment of more health maintenance organizations. Patients who sign up with these plans, either individually or through employers, pay a fee in advance and consult only with doctors who belong to the group, which offers comprehensive health care.

The idea of a prepaid group practice was introduced in the 1930s but was highly controversial. Some medical societies tried to have them declared illegal, but after 1941, the District of Columbia court ruled that this violated the Sherman Antitrust Act and said the AMA could not restrain trade in this way. Some states continued to restrict HMOs, even when the AMA voted in 1959 not to oppose prepaid group practices any longer.

In 1973, Congress enacted the Health Maintenance Organization Act to override such state restrictions. The act set federal standards for the organizations and said that any company with twenty-five or more employees is required to offer HMOs as an alternative to more conventional health plans if they are providing health insurance as a fringe benefit for their workers.

Enrollment grew rapidly during the 1980s. There was a 300 percent increase from 1979 to 1987, resulting in a total of 29.3 million by that year. Managed care plans between employers and care providers also rose steadily during the 1990s, reaching a 1993 total of about 53 percent of America's 256 million people. Among those who had health coverage through their jobs, 70 percent were in some kind of managed-care plan: 43 percent were in managed care fee-for-service plans, 18 percent were in HMOs, and 11 percent were in plans with negotiated payment rates. Employees have tended to switch to such plans when employers, hit by increasing insurance premiums, gave them the option of either paying the higher cost of an unlimited choice plan or accepting a cheaper prepaid one.

Studies have found that HMOs can reduce health care costs in similar populations, by 29 percent in one 1985 study.[8] Some of the requirements used by HMOs have spread to insurance carriers' plans: a second surgical opinion, preauthorization for hospital admission, more use of outpatient surgery, and limitations on testing.

A Variety of HMOs. A number of different health maintenance organizations have arisen around the country. Although they share many traits, they also have individual ways of meeting their goals of providing prepaid health care more efficiently.

One HMO, the Health Insurance Plan of Greater New York (HIP), began in 1947, growing to more than a million members by the 1990s. At forty-five affiliated medical group centers in the area, subscribers receive comprehensive care from general practitioners, pediatricians, obstetricians and gynecologists, and teams of specialists. They have no out-of-pocket payments because HIP eliminated deductibles (amounts that a patient must pay before insurance starts to pay for care) and co-insurance payments (those patients make for each service in addition to what insurance pays). With no claim forms, red tape and paperwork were greatly reduced.

The plan includes unlimited office and hospital visits, hospitalization benefits, maternity care, eye care and X-ray and lab work. Coverage also extends to physical exams, physical therapy, immunizations, injectable drugs, ambulance service, and visiting nurse services, but not to dental work, prescribed drugs, eyeglasses, artificial limbs, cosmetic surgery, alcohol or drug abuse treatment, and certain mental health care. Health educators in the organization aim to prevent illness.

The School of Public Health at Columbia University in New York City conducted a four-year study of different nonprofit medical and dental plans and said that HIP gave the most complete contract for health care in the state. The report praised HIP's high standards of care and extensive financial protection, praising the staff and low level of hospital admission rates.[9]

Another well-known HMO is the Kaiser Foundation Medical Care Program, which had its origins during the Depression of the 1930s. Construction workers in the southern California desert were located 200 miles (320 kilometers) from medical offices, so a small facility with a team of doctors was set up for them. The plan began with fees for services but changed to a prepaid plan costing $1.50 a month per person. In 1938, when Henry Kaiser began building the Grand Cooley Dam in Washington state, he set up a similar plan for his employees and their dependents.

The plan, costing fifty cents a week at the time, became Kaiser Foundation Health Plan and still includes Kaiser Industrial employees and their families (about 4 percent of the total) while many others—more than 3 million people in California, Oregon, Hawaii, Ohio, and Colorado—have joined. By the 1970s, this was the

A man holds up his Kaiser Permanente health plan card and his five dollar registration fee. The Kaiser Foundation Health Plan has grown into the largest HMO in the nation. Some people believe that managed-care networks such as this one are the wave of the future.

largest HMO in America, with more than 2,100 hospital beds and 1,500 doctors' offices. The program uses group practice and integrated facilities to enhance prevention and efficient care. It also offers people different kinds of plans.

Among the services covered are hospital care, physician services, anesthesia, eye exams, physical therapy, lab tests and X-rays, dressings, casts, special-duty nursing, up to twenty psychiatric visits, and maternity care (with a small added charge for a surgical delivery). Subscribers can buy drugs, medicines, allergy treatments, and injections at reduced rates. During the 1970s, people were not covered for dental care, drug addiction, self-inflicted problems, or for any transplants besides kidney.

The Xerox Corporation, a $17 billion dollar company with 55,000 employees in forty-seven states, has developed an employee health plan based on HMOs. The company screens HMOs for quality and service and negotiates contracts, often getting the HMOs to agree to limit their price increases, for example, keeping them at a rise of 5.5 percent in 1993. HMO costs per employee run approximately $3,846, while traditional care is much higher—$6,322 per active employee.

Xerox encourages employees to opt for these plans by paying a much larger share of the premium costs, and about two thirds of the employees have done so. They can choose from larger HMOs, such as Kaiser and U.S. Healthcare, or smaller, independent HMOs approved by the company, depending on where they live. Full family coverage in the HMO, including preventive checkups and expensive care such as fertility therapy, costs $239 a year. Despite the cost differential, some employees still prefer to choose their own doctors without any limitations. One twenty-nine-year-old employee pays $137.83 a month to cover her family, as well as paying a deductible, rather than joining the HMO, which would cost her only $20 a month.

Reactions to HMOs. Consumers have praised the convenience of having various health care services in one place. Some also think they are more likely to find a good doctor, because the HMO has already screened the people it hires, often relying on the opinions of other doctors. There is more continuity of care if a doctor moves away, and treatment can be planned more objectively, without any motivation to do a procedure in order to collect a fee. Costs to the employer are more predictable and the lack of claim forms pleases many. Comparison studies show there are fewer hospital admissions and surgeries among populations covered by HMOs.

Some HMO clients have complained about delays in getting appointments and trouble reaching their doctors by phone. Yet the waiting time for HMO appointments averaged twenty-one minutes during the 1970s, as opposed to thirty minutes for appointments made in advance and forty-five minutes for people who did not have appointments. Critics also warn that these organizations may practice "assembly line medicine" and not take as much interest in patients because they have a captive audience. Patients in HMOs tend to have fewer diagnostic tests and less specialty care.

In a poll taken in 1993, 17,000 Americans in a variety of settings were asked to rate their medical care. These results showed that patients liked HMOs the least, while ranking small-practice doctors highest. Patients of small-practice doctors were also more satisfied with explanations about their treatment and said their doctors were more concerned about their total health.[10] A Rand Corporation study of more than 600 patients suffering from depression found that those treated at HMOs did not improve as quickly or as much as those treated by doctors in private practice. As a rule, they received less ongoing care and less medication.[11]

Some physicians have said that doctors working in HMOs get less respect from their colleagues, which might discourage some top-quality people from choosing to work there. However, as more doctors join these managed care networks, such feelings are changing, especially among medical students and younger doctors.

Do HMOs help prevent health problems? Edmund Faltermayer says HMOs have "powerful financial reasons to keep you well."[12] Some go so far as to call people up encouraging them to have mammograms, prenatal care and classes, health classes, and blood pressure checks, for example.

Another version of prepaid care is the Preferred Provider Association (PPA), a network of independent care providers who agree to accept a reduced fee schedule. These have increased from a total of forty-two in 1982 to more than seven hundred in 1988. By then, more than 34 million people had health plans that included PPAs. Employers and some self-insured people have negotiated with these groups of providers for less expensive rates and have also worked out such arrangements with hospitals that have low occupancy rates. By joining a PPA, doctors and other health care providers can be guaranteed a certain amount of income each year, because of the prepayment involved.

Prepaid medical care has been called the wave of the future, something that will almost surely be a mainstay of the broader reforms being implemented during the 1990s. Some analysts say that even if the United States does not undertake sweeping reforms, prepayment is likely to be the only way the nation can afford health care. "It is the only system that incorporates incentives for provider efficiency," according to Don Holloway, director of management research and development at Stanford University Hospital. Holloway further says, "A system rewarded for keeping you well and satisfied could be a far better experience than one that is primarily interested in illness as a means of increasing revenue."[13]

As health care costs continued to spiral during the early 1990s, people have proposed various measures that call for more or less government involvement in health care. Rather than changing elements of health care facilities and delivery in one place or another, these changes would actually restructure the nation's health care system.

Models for Reform

As it became clear that America was ready for broad health care reforms, people began looking more closely at the health systems in different countries and at new programs being tried out in different states. Proposals began to circulate that offered solutions to the various problems besetting our health care system, especially its high costs.

What should Americans consider as they evaluate these different proposals? Theodore R. Marmor has summarized some goals that take into account the needs and wishes of many Americans. He said that people want:

- A system that will cover us all—rich, poor, employed, self-employed, unemployed....
- A system that will provide payment for all medically necessary care....
- A system that will be affordable for all of us, as individuals and as a nation.

- A system that will provide easily accessible, prompt, medically sound, and up-to-date care, respectfully delivered and even gratefully received.
- A system that will leave patients free to choose their doctors and hospitals, and leave doctors free to prescribe appropriate treatments.
- A system that will be user-friendly—indeed, provider friendly; a system without the forms and fine print on which bureaucracies flourish and people choke.
- A system in which providers of health care will be held accountable to consumers, payers, and society as a whole.
- A system that will be portable; that is, tied to a person, not to a job, company, or locale.[1]

No one plan can please everyone, but as Americans examine the different proposals, whether for single-payer systems, pay-or-play plans, or managed competition—these goals can illuminate the pros and cons of the various systems and their individual features. They show what trade-offs may occur, such as in having less choice for some in exchange for getting health coverage for all.

Incremental Reform. The idea behind incremental reform is to fine-tune the current system, leaving most of it intact. This plan has received support from many Republicans and some Democrats in Congress. The goal would be to bring insurance coverage to more people by helping small businesses purchase insurance from among currently existing plans. The government would not undertake to regulate health care or impose price controls. People would be encouraged to use more prepaid plans for health care—HMOs, PPOs, and the like. This would, it is hoped, result in more efficiency and

"Sorry, but under the New Health Reform Plan you can only get one opinion."

This doctor is voicing people's fear of the restrictions on health care services that may accompany reform.

competition in the marketplace. Incentives would be used to reduce and control costs.

A set of reforms proposed by House Minority Leader Robert Michel, a Republican from Illinois, would let employers make tax-exempt contributions to "Medi-Save" accounts for employees, who could then use the accounts to purchase supplemental insurance or pay medical expenses not covered by their regular plans. Self-employed people would be able to deduct all health insurance premiums. Michel's bill included some malpractice reform, requiring that claims first come before a mediation or arbitration board. Increased funding would be distributed for underserved rural areas and migrant worker health centers.

Single-Payer Model. Other nations—Japan, Canada, and many Western European countries—have developed a universal, standard payment system. Everyone in Canada, for example, has a health security card verifying their insurance through the government plan. These governments negotiate with doctors and hospitals, and in some cases drug manufacturers, to set fees and limit the amount they will spend on health care each year as a nation. Single-payer plans may involve private or government-run facilities.

The idea of a government-run system with a national health service has been unpopular with American lobbying groups and legislators through the years. When one such bill was introduced into Congress in the 1980s, only twenty representatives and not one senator supported it. The American Medical Association and the American Hospital Association were among those opposing it.

The single-payer Canadian system covers everyone, whether or not they are working. It is tax financed, so that people receive insurance through the government, not employers and insurance companies. They can choose from among (private) caregivers and hospitals, with the government regulating fees to control costs. At the province level, negotiations are conducted with political officials, drug companies, providers, and hospital administrators. Provinces receive government guidelines and run a sort of consumer cooperative, which receives federal funding to cover expenses.

Access to care is determined by how seriously ill a person is and who has the greatest need. All people are eligible for routine care on the same basis. Canada spends about 30 percent less per capita than the United States.

In this way, Canada has tried to balance the seemingly limitless desire people have for more and better care with the problem of costs. The media reports on these decisions as they are made and carried out by accountable public officials. Individual doctors make health-related decisions thereafter.

At present, America has a government-run, single-payer system with Medicare. The U.S. General Accounting Office has estimated that by using a single-payer plan for everything, the United States could save between $60 and $75 billion just on administrative costs.[2] A system in which a central office handled all paperwork and processed all claims might save enough to cover everyone now uninsured. About $160 billion is now spent on paperwork, so saving just half would yield about $80 billion.

But critics say that without controls or changes in the conventional fee-for-service system, costs could continue to rise with this plan. Strong incentives and heavy competition might be needed to control fees and limit the rate at which they rise.

Other critics say a single-payer system does not fully meet the needs of citizens. They point out that many Canadians come to the United States to get faster treatment and avoid the barriers or waiting lists they face in their own country. The premier of Quebec, Robert Bourassa, once went to Bethesda, Maryland, for surgery. Another Canadian, Al Hingley, waited fourteen months to receive triple-bypass surgery, although one artery to his heart was totally blocked and the other three were 99 percent clogged.[3] High-tech treatments are not as widely available in Canada, and there are far fewer innovations in research and pharmaceuticals.

Says Kevin Grumbach of the Health Access Coalition, "There is no perfect health system. I suppose that, if you are getting up there in age as a white male, it would be a hardship to wait for bypass surgery when you feel a twinge. But personally, I am willing to have that kind of hardship in return for getting health coverage for everyone. We have to decide what we want as a society."[4]

Still, many Americans don't think the government can run anything smoothly, especially health care: "I liked the equity of the Canadian system—I still do," says Walter Zelman, health care advisor to the insurance commissioner in California. "But I don't think Americans are willing to have the government run their health-care system. . . . If the government was in charge of health care, the question is, who would be governing who?"[5] Opponents also dislike the idea of forcing everyone to accept one idea of how to run a health care system.

Others say that America's best doctors would leave if a national health plan were implemented. They point out that some British physicians have relocated in America because they did not like the constraints in their government-run system. Theodore Marmor scoffs at this suggestion: "Where do these critics think they'd go? And a more subtle fear is being played upon here. It is that if we don't go on paying our doctors the exorbitant fees they currently enjoy, they will take their revenge on us, abandoning us when we are sick and helpless."[6]

Supporters of single-payer plans say criticism comes mostly from special interest groups who might lose money with this system because it controls costs better than others. Millions of dollars have been spent by lobbying groups representing insurers, drug companies, and doctors. Others who might lose jobs from this plan are people who work in the administration of insurance claims.

In 1992 New York began considering a single-payer system for the entire state. Other states, including Illinois, Missouri, Ohio, and Vermont, have also looked at instituting this reform. A Vermont poll in 1992 showed that 61 percent of the citizens there favored this type plan, which offers savings of time and money on paperwork. The Clinton health plan would let individual states develop single-payer plans in the context of the larger reforms.

Play-or-Pay. Under this plan, businesses must cover everyone or pay a certain payroll tax into a fund that would cover uninsured workers, the unemployed, and the poor. The payroll taxes could either go into a regional or a national fund. Unlike the single-payer plan, this one is based on employment, like the current U.S. system.

Objections to this plan are that employers may well decide not to take part, in which case the public program would be overloaded with people who are at the greatest risk of health problems. The government would have to offer a plan that competed strongly in terms of its quality and cost with the employer plans in order to give this plan a chance for success.

Managed Competition. A market-based reform, managed competition aims to encourage caregivers to decrease costs and increase efficiency. Its hallmarks are vigorous competition and a combination of free-market forces and some government intervention. Managed competition plans offer varying degrees of control, with some including spending caps and price controls while others view these as disastrous.

The most famous of these plans was originated by the Jackson Hole Group, a policy research group of insurers, providers, economists, corporate executives, and others that met at regular conferences in recent years in Wyoming. One group member, Dr. Alain Enthoven, a professor of economics at the Graduate School of Business at Stanford University, was its major architect. Enthoven helped Great Britain and the Netherlands to revamp their health care systems.

One of his ideas was to set up Health Insurance Purchasing Cooperatives (HIPCs) so that smaller businesses could join with larger groups to negotiate more successfully in the marketplace, among providers who have to compete for their business. These coalitions would include groups of employers and employees that negotiate with providers for the best care at the best price. There would be a standard package of insurance benefits for all, with tax exemptions just for these benefits. People would be expected to pay extra for benefits beyond this package.

Under this plan, consumers would have a choice of health plans, with providers giving information on their prices and even on the percentage of success of their procedures so that consumers could make informed choices. The key to managed competition is the use of prepaid plans for both doctors and hospitals. The system would reward those who showed the most skill, publicizing the results and comparing the different organizations. In these ways, the health care industry would contain more of the elements that are present when people buy other kinds of goods and services.

Critics of managed competition say it tries to do too much for everyone. Supporters of the single-payer plans complain that this is too similar to what already exists—more HMOs and other prepaid plans with no ceilings on costs. New bureaucracies might emerge with the HIPCs. And what about quality of care? "I am concerned about the assertion that a fixed fee per patient, independent of the amount of care provided, would encourage physicians to 'keep patients healthy and provide the most efficient care when they are sick.' " writes Dr. Wayne A. Bottner of La Crosse, Wisconsin. He says this may slow costs but not result in greater efficiency: "The concept of fixed reimbursement implies that the approach to the same problem in different patients need not vary to any great degree. This is simply not the case." Dr. Bottner worries that this system "creates a situation in which physicians and hospitals are tempted to shift focus from the patient's medical best interest to the system's fiscal best interest. . . . We must search for a system that encourages efficiency but not cutting corners."[7]

Comparing Other Systems. Countries with national health insurance include Japan (since 1922), most European nations, New Zealand, Australia, Canada, and Great Britain. In 1911 the British Parliament passed the first national health insurance act, which covered low-income workers, usually through membership in a health society. Later came coverage for all, through the National Health Service Act of 1946. After that, all hospital beds came under government control. Salaries for people in the health professions were regulated, and the system has kept costs lower than in the United States. In 1982 Americans spent 2.7 times more than Britain. Health care absorbed 5.9 percent of Britain's gross national product as opposed to 10.1 percent in the United States.

Through the National Health Service, the British receive services from primary care doctors, hospitals, and nurses regardless of where they live, their income, or social status. They cannot become destitute as a result of health care expenses.

Germany's system also rests on more government control, especially at times when costs are rising. A 1972 law gave the central government more say in planning and financing hospitals, and a 1976 law affected the distribution of primary care by planning the location of physicians. A year later, the parliament passed a new cost-containment law that authorized a group at the federal level to make annual decisions about health spending allotments. The government has influenced drug costs by ordering insurance funds to pay only the generic cost.

Health care providers negotiate with people who run what are called "sickness funds," started in the 1800s to cover workers. Employers pay for their employees while the government pays premiums for the elderly, unemployed, and indigent. All parties are expected to reach agreements that keep their costs within limits set by the federal guidelines.

Since 1946 all Britishers have been covered by government-controlled health care. This American woman lives in London, and so her daughter receives free health care under the British National Health Service.

German doctors administer their salaries from the fund. As of 1985, caps have been set on the annual total payments; doctors share the money depending on the amount of work each has done. Doctors may only start new practices in places where the government says there is a need. Most doctors make house calls. Emergency rooms are seldom as crowded as they are in urban U.S. areas.

Taking part in the sickness funds is now legally mandated for nearly 90 percent of all citizens, exempting the wealthy, who still do usually buy insurance. People can choose their doctors and hospitals, ranked among the world's best, and pay almost no fees themselves. Hospitalization costs about $400, with people paying $6 or $7 a day themselves. As in Canada, the most expensive high-tech equipment is located at teaching centers, not widely available. All citizens and foreign workers are covered.

Germany spends about half what America does on health care, slightly more than 8 percent of its gross national product. Unlike the U.S. system, there are fewer malpractice suits in Germany, and doctors do not use extraordinary measures to preserve life when a patient is viewed as terminally ill. An elderly person dying of natural causes would be given home care.

As costs have risen, the government has worked harder to pay hospitals less and encourage efficiency. A freeze was put on drug prices, along with an across-the-board reduction. Doctors were told to buy only generic drugs, if possible. The Germans also instigated something like the DRG system, paying for a given diagnosis or procedure, not the exact number of hospital days. There is pressure on caregivers, from a cost-conscious public, to keep prices down.

As in the United States, there is some debate about

how many benefits should apply to every person and also about nursing-home care. The costs of the latter are similar to that in America, and some children have been forced to pay for the care of invalid parents who had no money. Germany has considered a new state-run insurance program for this kind of long-term care.

Some people have called the Japanese system the most efficient in the world. Unlike Canada and Germany, which have private doctors, the Japanese government owns hospitals and clinics, which are generally crowded and less physically attractive than those in America. There may be long waits to see a doctor, and doctors spend less time with individuals, often not explaining the details of their diagnosis or treatment plans. People also complain that doctors prescribe too many medications, which they buy themselves and sell to patients at a profit. New laws may end that practice.

Yet the Japanese enjoy high levels of health, perhaps due in part to their healthier low-fat and low-sugar diets. The life expectancy is 75.9 for men and 81.8 for women, the highest in the world. Infant mortality is only 0.46 per live births. Of course, the population is more homogeneous than America's, with few indigent people. Malpractice claims are rare.

However, like other industrialized countries, Japan has growing numbers of elderly who use a great deal of health care and medications. Their number will double in about twenty years. New health care costs are expected to be borne by the taxpayers rather than by Japan's corporations. Now health care premiums are deducted from people's paychecks and cost an average of 2.7 percent of their salaries, a sum that is matched by their employers.

"In Japan, there is real equality. That is our

A little girl watches expectant mothers in a "maternitybics" class at a government-run clinic in Tokyo. Although there are complaints about the quality of care in Japan, the system is one of the most efficient in the world.

strength," said Dr. Naoki Ikegami, health administrator at Keio University School of Medicine. "You get your money's worth in the United States, but if you don't have the money, you don't get the worth."[8]

People think it unlikely that America would adopt the Japanese system, considering its much larger size, diversity of regions, higher poverty, and strong health industry lobbies. There are also objections to the systems used in Canada and elsewhere: less convenient access to high technology and waiting lists for complicated surgeries. What plan makes the best sense for a pluralistic society like America, with its history of individualism and entrepreneurialism? How will the diverse groups working on the issue—politicians and their constituents, health care providers, insurers, hospital administrators, and economists—find common ground?

Prospects for the Future

"Clinton Offering Health Plan With Guarantee of Coverage and Curb on Private Spending," announced news headlines in September 1993. That month, as he addressed Congress and the American people, President Clinton said that the nation's health care system was "badly broken, and it is time to fix it."

Americans had been eagerly awaiting the details of the president's health care reform plan. For months, Hillary Rodham Clinton and the Health Care Task Force had been gathering information and discussing reforms. Now people wanted to know how the president intended to provide coverage to all Americans, reduce health care costs, and calm people's fears about the future.

Clinton's plan, called "The American Health Security Act of 1993," proposed changes in the way health care was funded and delivered. It included many elements of managed competition and kept the traditional employment-based insurance coverage. This coverage would pay for the services of health care providers organized in HMOs or other kinds of networks.

First Lady Hillary Rodham Clinton meets members of the Forum on Health Care Reform in 1993. As head of the Health Care Task Force, she was responsible for developing the plan that President Bill Clinton presented to Congress.

The health care plans offered by any provider organization, whether HMO, insurance company, or network, would have to be approved by the state and by a regional alliance, a cooperative buying service that would act on behalf of consumers in each region. Consumers would be responsible for choosing a plan, based on their needs, location, prices, and other factors, and would then purchase a plan from the alliance.

A guaranteed national benefit package designed by the Task Force includes services that are "medically necessary or appropriate," following a list that includes: care by physicians and other authorized health care givers; family planning and pregnancy related services; and more preventive care than has typically been the case for many insurance policies—immunizations, routine physical exams, preventive dental care for children up to age eighteen, vision and hearing exams, and some routine testing, to be recommended by a National Health Board, as well as health education classes. Other items covered include thirty outpatient visits and thirty inpatient days for mental health care; treatment for substance abuse, ambulances, emergency services, hospital care, home health care, hospice care, prescription drugs, medical equipment such as prosthetics, lab and X-ray services, and up to 100 days in a nursing home or rehabilitation hospital a year.

Who Pays? Under this plan, employers would provide coverage for all their full-time workers, at least 80 percent of the cost of premiums in their region. Employees would pay the remaining 20 percent as well as any required deductibles and co-payments for specific kinds of care. If they chose a more expensive plan than the basic one, they would pay more for that. Part-time employees would pay a pro-rated share of premiums covered by their employers, and self-employed people would pay a tax-deductible amount that is "capped," because they are considered as small businesses.

Unemployed people would have to pay for health insurance on their own unless they qualified for what is now called Medicaid, Medicare, or a low-income subsidy for people whose incomes fall below 150 percent of the poverty level (set at $14,300 a year for a family of four and $7,100 for individuals).

In order to cover everyone, the government would need to raise more money, which the Clinton plan said could come partly from a new tax on cigarettes. Deductible medical expenses would also be lower, which would bring in more taxes. Savings in federal health programs (for example, a plan to cap Medicare spending and thus save $100 billion) and in administration of health care would be expected to pay the rest. The nation's total payroll was about $3.6 trillion in 1993. If all employers paid about 7 percent, the total would add up to $250 billion a year.

Some critics have said that these amounts would still not cover all the costs if the plan took effect in 1997. Republican pollster Tony Fabrizio said, "Nobody will believe him [Clinton] when he says that this won't cost you."[1] A number of Americans have also voiced fears that there would be higher taxes to pay for such a comprehensive plan. Many are aware that other countries with universal health programs have higher taxes; for instance, Canadians pay 13 percent more in taxes than Americans do.

The mandate that small businesses provide insurance has been opposed as well. Critics say that many such businesses will be forced to close because they cannot afford insurance, with job losses as a result. Clinton has proposed limiting the expenditures of businesses that employ fewer than seventy-five people to no more than 7.9 percent of payroll. Some subsidies could also be put in place to help these businesses phase in coverage, especially for low-income workers.

Quality Issues. President Clinton stated a need "to keep what is good about our health care system." His plan suggested ways for people to learn more about health care quality through reports by the regional alliances, including "quality performance reports." Each year, consumers could choose a different plan if they were not satisfied with the one they were in. People could also switch plans at any time with just cause.

States would be responsible for quality analysis, through licensing health care providers, as it does now, and by authorizing the different health plans offered in its borders. Each alliance would have an office to handle problems and complaints, which might reduce the incidence of malpractice suits.

Access. Under Clinton's plan, everyone would have insurance that was bought through the health alliances, so people would not be labeled as Medicaid versus private patients. The National Health Board would oversee the states' plans to make health care available to legal residents in their borders. The Indian Health Service would remain much the same and could get more funding, as might services in remote and underserved areas.

Local boards would consider the availability of expensive equipment, hospital beds, and technology. The goal would be to have enough available in a given area, but to prevent technology from becoming too concentrated or needless. The competition involved would help to ensure efficiency and to avoid the overuse of tests and procedures.

The public debate intensified as details of health care reform were being worked out. People who had little interest in the subject have learned more about how the system works and how it might work differently. People are evaluating the elements new plans might include and how they would affect their own lives and communities.

Many analysts warn that there is no quick cure for the nation's health care system and that some trade-offs are inevitable. The Clinton plan proposed that a limit be put on how much America as a whole spends on health care each year. This bothers many individuals and groups such as the Coalition for Health Care Choices, which also opposes mandatory health alliances and a flat community rating in which everyone pays the same premium regardless of lifestyle or health habits.[2]

Journalist Chris Powell notes that the demand for services is potentially infinite while resources are limited: "Rationing is the only way to make health care universal without committing all the nation's resources to it. . . . If costs are to be controlled even as health care is to be extended to those who lack it, society has to choose, say, between expensive treatments for the few and inexpensive treatments for the many, between, say, an 85-year-old's hip replacement and vaccinations for hundreds of children."[3]

Along those lines, author Robert J. Samuelson says, "Even if tough cost controls ended all waste, there remains a more basic source of rising health spending: expensive new medical technologies. Lower spending in Canada and other countries . . . partly reflects limits on technology. The journal *Health Affairs* reports that six new technologies are generally two to seven times more available in the United States than in Canada or West Germany. . . . But rationing Americans' access to new technologies would provoke loud protests."[4] Samuelson is among those who say that Americans have unrealistic expectations.

Don Hollaway points out, "Under the traditional. . . . structures that tend to reward volume, society can expect medical creativity and innovation, speedy development and application of new treatments, some marginal or unnecessary procedures—and rapidly escalating costs that now fall disproportionately on employers' shoulders." In a prepaid system, he says, "Providers would have more interest in research and programs that keep people well and away from the more expensive part of the system. Since a great number of medical problems are related to life style, that change alone could improve the nation's health, in particular that of indigent people, who are ignored until they need emergency treatment."[5]

Dr. William B. Schwartz of the University of Southern California also sees tough choices ahead. "Twenty years ago, when making ward rounds with my students, I'd say that we'll go on trying the next test or treatment and the next one until there is no hope of helping the patient. If we want to continue to teach that philosophy, it's going to be incredibly costly."[6] He is among those who say some kind of rationing is needed if health care costs are to go down. These critics believe that other nations have already faced the reality that no country can do all that it would like to for its citizens.

At the same time, many people see opportunities to make the American system simpler, more equitable, and more effective. There is a renewed emphasis on prevention of illness. This pleases people who believe America's health services need to shift from concentrating on acute illnesses to chronic diseases and continuous forms of care. Author Aubrey McTaggart sees a need to move "from the concept of sick care to well care."[7]

There is also more interest in taking individual responsibility to safeguard our health as much as possible. The government will likely take on an even larger role in public education, as well as providing community screening programs, issuing warnings about health risks, controlling what drugs and foods are approved, and urging people to avoid risky behaviors, such as smoking and abusing alcohol and drugs.

People may also learn under what conditions a medical visit is really necessary. At present, many people seek treatment for colds and minor problems or illnesses that do not have a cure or require intervention. One study showed that most doctor visits were for transient upper respiratory infections and gastroenteritis (such as indigestion and intestinal flu) with nothing else being wrong. People may think the right pill will cure them, when they actually have a virus that cannot be cured by medication. Some chronic health problems do not improve with medical treatment. Knowledge about the limits of conventional medical science would help people to have more reasonable expectations.

In the meantime, people continue to debate the political, economic, and moral implications of reforming America's health care system. The plan that emerges after this spirited debate will be an attempt to balance different interests and to bring health care to more than 270 million people in a way that does not cripple the nation's economy and keeps American health care second to none.

Appendix

*On the facing page is a list of
elements that all health care plans
need to address.*

*These criteria, published by the
League of Women Voters Education Fund
and the Henry J. Kaiser Family Foundation,
can be used to analyze the various
health care reform bills.*

1. General Approach
2. Coverage
3. Scope of Coverage Pools
4. Benefits
5. Federal Costs
6. Effect on Overall National Health Costs
7. Federal Financing
8. Premiums, Cost-Sharing, and Out-of-Pocket Payments
9. Tax Treatment of Health Insurance
10. Cost Containment
11. Federal Administration
12. Provider Reimbursement
13. Phase-in of Coverage
14. Coverage of Older Persons
15. Coverage of Low-Income Persons
16. Coverage of Persons with Disabilities
17. Treatment of Medicare
18. Treatment of Medicaid
19. Reforms in Health Insurance
20. Reforms in Health Care Access
21. Reforms in Health Professions Education
22. Managed Care
23. Quality
24. Protections for Individuals
25. Malpractice Reform

Source Notes

Chapter One

1. Peter T. Kilborn, "American Voices on Health Care: Even in Security, Anxiety," *The New York Times,* May 9, 1993, sec. A, p. 20 (also includes interviews with Debra O'Connor, William and Gertrude Coen; and Maria Weirather).
2. Ibid.
3. Richard L. Berke, "First Lady Promotes Health-Care Plan," *The New York Times,* May 2, 1993, sec. A, p. 40.
4. Stephen J. Williams and Sandra J. Guerra, *A Consumer's Guide to Health Care Services* (Englewood Cliffs, N.J.: Prentice Hall, 1985), p. 9.
5. Michael Duffy and Dick Thompson, "Behind Closed Doors," *Time,* September 20, 1993, p. 63.

Chapter Two

1. Statistics from U.S. Bureau of the Census. *Historical Statistics of the United States, Colonial Times to 1970: Bicentennial Edition, Part 1.* Washington, D.C., Government Printing Office, 1975, Table B, 126–135.

Chapter Three

1. Quoted in Suzanne M. Coil, *The Poor in America* (New York: Julian Messner, 1989), p. 28.

2. H. Jack Geiger, "Community Health Centers: Health Care as an Instrument of Social Change," in Victor W. Sidel and Ruth Sidel, *Reforming Medicine: Lessons of the Last Quarter Century.* (New York: Random House, 1984), p. 15.
3. "Rural Doctor Program Is Flawed, Study Says," *The New York Times,* September 27, 1992, sec. A, p. 30.
4. Geiger, p. 13.
5. Odin W. Anderson, "Health Services in the United States: A Growth Enterprise for a Hundred Years," in Theodor Litman and Leonard S. Robins, eds., *Health Politics and Policy* (New York: John Wiley and Sons, 1984), p. 75.
6. Robin Toner, "Poll on Changes in Health Care Finds Support Amid Skepticism," September 22, 1993, p. A-1.
7. Robert Pear, "Its Eye on Election, White House to Propose Health Care Changes," *The New York Times,* November 12, 1991, sec. A, p. 1.
8. Robin Toner, "How Much Health-Care Reform Will the Patient Go Along With?" *The New York Times,* March 7, 1993, sec. 4, p. 1.

Chapter Four

1. Shirley Streshinsky, "Can You Afford to Get Sick?" *Glamour,* September 1992, p. 303.
2. Robert Samuelson, "Health Care: How We Got Into This Mess," *Newsweek,* October 4, 1993, p. 31.
3. Gina Kolata, "Catch-22: Lose Health, Lose Policy," *The New York Times,* November 14, 1993, sec. 4-A, p. 4.
4. Howard H. Hiatt, M.D., *America's Health in the Balance: Choice or Chance* (New York: Harper and Row, 1987), p. xi.
5. Quoted in Geiger, p. 12.
6. Streshinsky, p. 336.
7. Streshinsky, p. 336.
8. James Rosenthal, "The Great Health Debate," *Harper's Bazaar,* October 1992, p. 204.
9. Barry Meier, "Is Your Health Insurance Safe?" *Reader's Digest,* June 1992, p. 92.
10. Meier, p. 95.

11. Eli Ginsberg, *The Limits of Health Reform: The Search for Realism* (New York: Basic Books, 1977), p. 30.
12. James R. Knickman and Kenneth E. Thorpe, "Financing for Health Care," in Kovner, Anthony R. et al. *Health Care Delivery in the United States,* 4th ed. (New York: Springer, 1990), p. 264.
13. Elisabeth Rosenthal, "Confusion, Errors, and Fraud in Medical Bills," *The New York Times,* November 14, 1993, sec. 4-A, p. 5.
14. Ibid.
15. Statistics from the Association of American Medical Colleges, cited in Elisabeth Rosenthal, "Too Few General Doctors," *The New York Times,* November 14, 1993, sec. 4-A, p. 6.
16. Ibid.
17. Hiatt, p. 24.
18. Samuelson, "Health Care: How We Got Into This Mess," p. 34.
19. Statistics from *Consumer Reports* "The 'Crisis' that Isn't: Malpractice: A Straw Man," July 1992, p. 443.
20. Samuelson, "Health Care: How We Got Into This Mess," p. 35.
21. Samuelson, "Health Care: How We Got Into This Mess," p. 32.
22. "Wasted Health-Care Dollars," *Consumer Reports,* July 1992, p. 441.
23. Rand Corporation studies cited in Thorpe, Kenneth, "Health Care Cost Containment," p. 274.
24. "The $200-Billion Bottom Line," *Consumer Reports,* July 1992, pp. 436–37.
25. Elisabeth Rosenthal, "Exploring the Murky World of Drug Prices," *The New York Times,* March 26, 1993, sec. E-3.
26. Ibid.
27. Lawrence K. Altman, "Cost of Treating AIDS Patients Is Soaring," *The New York Times,* July 23, 1992, sec. B, p. 8.
28. "The $200-Billion Bottom Line," *Consumer Reports,* July 1992, pp. 436–37.

29. Gwen Ifill, "Clinton Asserts Health Plan Will Solve Red-Tape Crisis," *The New York Times*, September 18, 1993, sec. A, p. 6.
30. Harold Hornstein, "Clinton Health Plan Slated for Hearing at Local Forum," *Westport News*, September 24, 1993, p. A-12.

Chapter Five

1. Rosenthal, "The Great Health Debate," p. 203.
2. Ibid.
3. Thomas J. Bole III and William Bondeson, *Rights to Health Care* (Dordrecht, the Netherlands: Kluwer Academic Publishers, 1991), p. 2.
4. Ibid.
5. "Medicine Responds to President Clinton: A Statement from Lonnie R. Bristow, M.D., Chairman Board of Trustees, The American Medical Association," Chicago, Ill.: AMA, September 22, 1993, unpaged.
6. Hiatt, p. 8.
7. Hiatt p. 26.
8. Constance Matthiessen, "Code Blue," *Mother Jones*, November/December 1992, p. 62.
9. Geiger, p. 16.
10. AMA Council on Medical Service, "Quality of Care." *The Journal of the American Medical Association*, August 1986, Volume 256, p. 1032.

Chapter Six

1. "Wasted Health-Care Dollars," p. 436.
2. Edmund Faltermayer, "A Health Plan That Can Work," *Fortune*, June 14, 1993, pp. 89–90.
3. Elisabeth Rosenthal, "Exploring the Murky World of Drug Prices," *The New York Times*, March 26, 1993, sec. E-3.
4. Geiger, p. 30.
5. Letter to the Editor, *The New York Times*, May 6, 1992, op-ed.

6. Aubrey C. McTaggart and Lorna M. McTaggart, *The Health Care Dilemma,* 2nd ed. (Boston: Allyn and Bacon, 1971) p. 141.
7. Quoted in Elisabeth Rosenthal, sec. E-3.
8. Anthony R. Kovner, et al. *Health Care Delivery in the United States,* 4th ed. (New York: Springer, 1990) p. 282.
9. Ibid.
10. "Patients Tell of HMO Woes," *First,* November 1, 1993, p. 20A.
11. Ibid.
12. Faltermayer, p. 91.
13. Don Holloway, "Prepaid Medical Care: The Heart of Any Reform," *The New York Times,* April 21, 1993, sec. A, p. 23, op. ed.

Chapter Seven

1. Theodore R. Marmor, "Strong Medicine," *Lear's,* February 1993, p. 18.
2. Health Care Strategy Network. "Health Care Reform in the Clinton Administration: What Does It Mean?" A National Conference for Journalists, Columbia University, March 1993, unpaged.
3. Letter to the editor. *The New York Times,* August 13, 1992, edit. page.
4. Matthiessen, p. 32.
5. Ibid.
6. Marmor, p. 22.
7. Letter to the editor, *The New York Times,* August 13, 1992, op. ed.
8. James Sterngold, "Japan's Health Care: Cradle, Grave, and No Frills," *The New York Times,* December 28, 1992, sec. A, p. 8.

Chapter Eight

1. Quoted in "Watch the Numbers," *Business Week,* September 20, 1993, p. 32.

2. Coalition for Health Insurance Choices, "Health Care Reform Made Simple," unpaged, 1993.
3. Chris Powell, "Universal Health Care and the Politicians," *Westport News,* October 17, 1990, p. A 24.
4. Robert J. Samuelson, "The Cost of Chaos," *Newsweek,* October 2, 1989, p. 52.
5. Holloway, p. sec. A, p. 23, op ed.
6. Erik Eckholm, "Those Who Pay Health Costs Think About Drawing Lines," *The New York Times,* March 28, 1993, sec. 4, p. 1.
7. McTaggart and McTaggart, p. 5

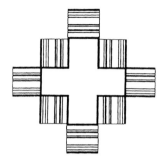

Bibliography

Articles

Abramowitz, K.S. "The Future of Health Care in America." *MGM Journal,* July/August 1988, pp. 42ff.

Belkin, Lisa. "Doctor Fears Changes May Be for Worse." *The New York Times,* May 13, 1993, sec A, p. 1; sec. B, p. 6.

Berke, Richard L. "First Lady Promotes Health-Care Plan." *The New York Times,* May 2, 1993, sec. A, p. 40.

"Clapping For Health Reform." (Editorial) *The New York Times,* September 24, 1993, sec. A, p. 32.

Clymer, Adam. "Clinton Offering Health Plan With Guarantee of Coverage and Curb on Private Spending." *The New York Times,* September 11, 1993, sec. A, pp. 1, 10.

Coyle, Joseph, et. al. "Who Wins Under Clinton's Health Care Plan?" *Money,* May 1993, pp. 98–105.

Duffy, Michael and Dick Thompson. "Behind Closed Doors." *Time,* September 20, 1993, pp. 60–63.

Dyer, Paula and Garland, Susan B. "A Roar of Discontent." *Business Week,* November 25, 1991, pp. 28–30.

Eckholm, Erik. "A Benefit for Some Patients, Difficult Choices for Others." *The New York Times,* September 11, 1993, sec. A, pp. 1, 10.

———. "Study Links Paperwork to 25% of Hospital Costs." *The New York Times*, August 6, 1993, sec. B, p. 1.

———. "Those Who Pay Health Costs Think About Drawing Lines." *The New York Times*, March 28, 1993, sec. 4, p. 1.

Freudenheim, Milt. "On Health Insurance, Some States Are Going Back to Basics." *The New York Times*, April 26, 1992, sec. E, p. 5.

Goodgame, Tom. "Ready to Operate." *Time*, Sept 20, 1993, pp. 49–54.

"Health Care Overhaul Is Approved in Oregon." *The New York Times*, August 6, 1993, sec. A, p. 18.

"HMOs: Are They the Answer to Your Medical Needs?" *Consumer Reports*, 39, October, 1974, p. 756.

Don Holloway. "Prepaid Medical Care: The Heart of Any Reform." *The New York Times*, April 21, 1992, sec. A, p. 23.

Hubner, John. "The Abandoned Father of Health Care Reform." *The New York Times*, July 18, 1993, sec. A, pp. 25–29.

Kerr, Peter. "Elderly Care: The Insurers' Role." *The New York Times*, March 16, 1993, sec. D, p. 1.

Kilborn, Peter T. "American Voices on Health Care: Even in Security, Anxiety" *The New York Times*, May 9, 1993, sec. A, pp. 1, 20.

Krauss, Clifford. "Lobbyists of Every Stripe on Health Care Proposal." *The New York Times*, September 24, 1993, sec. A, pp. 1, 20.

McNamee, Mike. "Health Care: Just Address the Bills to Corporate America," *Business Week*, March 29, 1993, pp. 66–68.

Marmor, Theodore R. "Strong Medicine." *Lear's*, February 1993, pp. 18–22.

Matthiessen, Constance. "Health Care." *Mother Jones*, November/December 1992, pp. 26–32; pp. 62 ff.

Meier, Barry. "Is Your Health Insurance Safe?" *Reader's Digest*, June 1992, pp. 97–111.

Morganthau, Tom, et al. "The Clinton Solution." *Newsweek*, September 20, 1993, pp. 31–35.

Pear, Robert. "Health Plan Would Penalize Excessive Drug Pricing." *The New York Times*, September 10, 1993, sec. A, p. 17.

———. "Health Planners at White House Consider Lid on Medicare Costs." *The New York Times*, August 30, 1993, sec. A, pp. 1, 14.

———. "Levy on Payrolls for Health Care Gathers Support." *The New York Times*, May 6, 1993, sec. A, pp. 1, 23.

———. "Medicare and Medicaid Cutback of $238 Billion Is Envisioned." *The New York Times*, September 9, 1993, sec. A, pp. 1, 22.

———. "Officials Predict Deluge of Suits On Health Plan." *The New York Times*, September 27, 1993, sec. A, pp. 1, 8.

Priest, Dana. "A Health Care Primer." *Washington Post*, March 9, 1993, sec. A, pp. 1, 11.

Protzman, Ferdinand. "Germany Approves Sweeping Health Care Reform." *The New York Times*, December 20, 1992, sec. A, p. 8.

Rosenthal, Elisabeth. "Exploring the Murky World of Drug Prices," *The New York Times*, March 26, 1993, sec. E-3.

Rosenthal, James. "The Great Health Debate." *Harper's Bazaar*, October 1992, pp. 202–205.

Samuelson, Robert J. "The Cost of Chaos." *Newsweek*, October 2, 1989, p. 52.

———. "Nationalize Health Care." *Newsweek*, October 26, 1992, p. 50.

Sterngold, James. "Japan's Health Care: Cradle, Grave, and No Frills." *The New York Times,* December 28, 1992, sec. A, pp. 1, 8.

Streshinsky, Shirley. "Can You Afford to Get Sick?" *Glamour,* September 1992, pp. 303, 334–337.

Whitney, Craig R. "Health Care Evolves as Issue In Britain's General Election." *The New York Times,* March 28, 1992, sec. A, pp. 1, 6.

———. "Medical Care in Germany: With Choices, and For All." *The New York Times,* January 23, 1993, sec. A, pp. 1, 4.

Books and Pamphlets

ABC National News Survey. Storrs, Conn.: Roper Center, University of Connecticut. July 8, 1984; October 28, 1985.

American Hospital Association. *Hospital Statistics.* (1988 edition) Chicago: American Hospital Association, 1988, p. xxvi.

American Nurses Association. *Nursing Association Policy.* Kansas City, Mo.: ANA, 1980.

Andreopoulos, Spyros. *National Health Insurance: What Can We Learn from Canada?* New York: John Wiley and Sons, 1975.

Bole, Thomas J., III and William Bondeson. *Rights to Health Care.* Dordrecht, the Netherlands: Kluwer Academic Publishers, 1991.

Brown, Lawrence D. *Health Policy in the United States: Issues and Options.* New York: The Ford Foundation, 1988.

———. *The Political Structure of the Health Planning System.* Washington, D.C.: Brookings Institution, 1982.

Callahan, James J., Jr. and Stanley S. Wallack, eds. *Reforming the Long-Term Care System.* Lexington, Mass.: D.C. Heath, 1981.

Esselstyn, Caldwell B. "Group Practice as Solution," in U.S. Department of Health, Education, and Welfare, Public Health Service-Labor Seminar on Consumer Health Services (Washington, D.C.: U.S. Government Printing Office, 1968), pp. 38–39.

Feder, Judith, and John Holahan and Theodore Marmor. *National Health Insurance: Conflicting Goals and Policy Choices.* Washington, D.C.: Urban Institute, 1980.

Fein, Rashi. *Medical Care, Medical Costs.* Cambridge, Mass.: Harvard University Press, 1986.

Ginsberg, Eli. *The Limits of Health Reform: The Search for Realism.* New York: Basic Books, 1977.

William Glaser, *Paying the Hospital: Foreign Lessons.* United States Center for the Social Sciences, Columbia University, December 1979.

Hall, J.K. et al. *One Hundred Years of American Psychiatry.* New York: Columbia University Press, 1947.

Hiatt, Howard H., M.D. *America's Health in the Balance: Choice or Chance.* New York: Harper and Row, 1987.

Knowles, John H. "The Hospital" in Stephen J. Williams. *Issues in Health Services.* New York: John Wiley, 1980.

Kovner, Anthony R. et al. *Health Care Delivery in the United States.* 4th ed. New York: Springer, 1990.

Lindorff, Dave. *Marketplace Medicine: The Rise of the For-Profit Hospital Chains.* New York: Bantam Books, 1992.

Litman, Theodor and Leonard S. Robins, eds. *Health Politics, and Policy.* New York: John Wiley and Sons, 1984.

McTaggart, Aubrey C. and Lorna M. McTaggart. *The Health Care Dilemma.* 2nd ed. Boston: Allyn and Bacon, 1971.

Maxwell, Robert J. *Health and Wealth: An International Study of Health Care Spending.* Lexington, Mass.: Lexington Books, 1981.

National Health Insurance: Hearings Before the Committee on Labor and Public Welfare, U.S. Senate. 91st Cong. 2d sess. Washington, D.C.: Government Printing Office, 1970.

Pierce, R.M. *Long Term Care for the Elderly: A Legislator's Guide.* Washington, D.C.: National Conference of State Legislatures and the American Association of Retired Persons, 1987.

President's Commission on Mental Health. *Report to the President 1978.* Washington, D.C.: U.S. Government Printing Office, 1978.

Roemer, Milton I. *National Health Systems of the World: Vol. One: The Countries.* New York: Oxford University Press, 1991.

Schramm, Carl J., ed. *Health Care and Its Costs.* New York: W.W. Norton, 1987.

Sidel, Victor W. and Ruth Sidel, *Reforming Medicine: Lessons of the Last Quarter Century.* New York: Random House, 1984.

Somers, Herman M. and Anne R. Somers. *Doctors, Patients, and Health Insurance.* Washington, D.C.: The Brookings Institution, 1961.

Talbott, J.A. ed. *State Mental Hospitals: Problems and Potentials.* New York: Human Sciences Press, 1980.

United States Department of Health, Education, and Welfare. *Health Planning and Resources Development Act of 1974.* Washington. D.C.: U.S. Government Printing Office, 1974.

———. *Hill Burton Is . . .* Washington, D.C.: U.S. Government Printing Office, 1972.

———. *Report to the President and Congress on the Status of Health Personnel in the United States.* (Vol. 1.) DHHS Pub. No. HRS P-OD 84-4) Washington, D.C.: DHHS 1984.

United States Senate Special Committee on Aging. *Nursing Home Care: The Unfinished Agenda.* Staff Report, May 21, 1986.

Williams, Stephen J. and Sandra J. Guerra, *A Consumer's Guide to Health Care Services,* Englewood Cliffs, N.J.: Prentice Hall, 1985.

Yale, Geoffrey. *The High Cost of Health: A Patient's Guide to the Hazards of Medical Politics.* Toronto: James Lorimar and Co., 1987.

Index

Page numbers in *italics* refer to illustrations.

Access to health care, 16, 23, 49, 72, 74-80, 82, 83, 87, 122
Accident insurance, 31
AIDS epidemic, 46, 59, 69, 70, 72, *73*, 76, 82, 94
Alzheimer's disease, 68, 94
American Association of Retired Persons (AARP), 47-48
American Health Security Act of 1993, 118, 120-124
American Hospital Association (AHA), 45, 106
American Medical Association (AMA), 32, 35, 45, 76, 83, 95, 106
Australia, 79, 93, 111

Birth weight, 17
Blacks, 36, 37, 79
Blue Cross/Blue Shield, 18, 30, 31, 51, 53

Board certification, 84

Canada, 17, 58, 75, 79, 93, 106-108, 111, 117, 121
Carter, Jimmy, 44
Catastrophic coverage, 12, 18, 47
CAT (computerized axial tomography) scanners, 65, *66*
Childbirth, 24, 28, 90
Clerical functions, 27-28
Clinton, Bill, *11*, 13, 76, 85, 92, 109, 118, 122
Clinton, Hillary Rodham, 13, 17, 22, 118, *119*
Co-insurance, 96-97
Committee on the Costs of Medical Care, 35
Community health centers, 43
Community rating legislation, 91-92
Consortiums, 90

Deductibles, 96
Dental care, 59, 76, 120

(141)

Diagnostic Related Groups (DRGs), 89-90, 114
Diagnostic tests, 12, 19, 65, 66, 92-93, 122
Drug and alcohol abuse, 46, 76, 120

Elderly population, 17, 35, 36, 39, 46, 61, 115
Emergency rooms, 18, 37, 77-78, 80, 114, 120
Employment-based insurance coverage, 12, 14-15, 31, 47, 55, 106, 109, 118
Epidemics, 24

Fair Labor Standards Act, 61
Family planning, 59, 120
Federal deficit, 46, 48
Fee-for-service basis, 46
France, 79

Germany, 17, 30, 58, 112, 114-115
Germ theory, 25
Glaser, Elizabeth, 72, *73*
Great Britain, 17, 30, 62, 75, 79, 108-109, 111-112, *113*
Great Depression, 28, 35
Great Society, 36-37

Health care costs, 17-19, 44-47, 58-64
   development of insurance, 30-31
   efforts to control, 86-102
   fraud, waste, and abuse, 69, 71
   medications, 67-69, 93-95
   postwar concerns, 31-33
   procedures and surgery, 65, 67, 92-93
Health care reform, 10, 19, 21-22, 39, 45, 47, 76-79, 84-85, 94, 103-125
Health care system, evolution of, 17-18, 23-35
Health Insurance Purchasing Cooperatives (HIPCs), 110
Health maintenance organizations (HMOs), 45, 46, 86, 95-97, *98*, 99-101
Health Manpower Act of 1971, 41
Health Professions Educational Assistance Act of 1976, 41
Heart surgery, 56, *57*, 67, 68, 79
Hill-Burton Act (Hospital Survey and Construction Act) of 1946, 31-33
Hispanics, 37, 79
HIV (human immunodeficiency virus), 69
Home care, 28, 76, 114, 120
Hospice care, 76, 120

Immunizations, 26, 28, 37, *38*, 79
Impersonality of health care, 84
Incremental reform, 104, 106
Infant mortality, 16-17, 37, 79, 115

Inflation, 16, 17, 58, 59
Israel, 79

Japan, 17, 58, 75, 106, 111, 115, *116*, 117
Johnson, Lyndon B., 36-37

Kaiser Foundation Medical Care Program, 97, *98*, 99
Kennedy, Edward M., 19
Kennedy, John F., 39, 43

League of Women Voters, 92
Life expectancy, 16, 25, 37, 115
Long-term care, 61, 76

Malpractice, 19, 63-64, 106, 115
Managed care services, 45, 46, 95-97, 99-101
Managed competition, 110-111, 118
Medicaid, 10, 13, 18, 39, 44-47, 59, 69, 80, 86
Medical schools, 35, 40
Medical technology, 16, 17, 48, 49, 59, 65, *66*, 67, 79, 122-124
Medicare, 10, 15, 18, 39, 44-47, 59, 62, 69, 86, 107, 121
Medicare Catastrophic Act of 1988, 47-48
Medications, 67-69, 93-95
Medigap, 47
Mental health care, 32, 43-44, 76, 120

Mental Retardation Facilities and Community Mental Health Construction Act of 1963, 43
Military health care, 32-33, 43
MRI (magnetic resonance imaging) machines, 65

National Health Board, 120, 122
National health care (*see* Universal health care)
National Health Service Corps, 41, *42*
National Health Service (Great Britain), 30, 111-112, *113*
National Institute of Mental Health, 43
National Institutes of Health, 35
National Mental Health Act of 1946, 43
Native Americans, 24, 37
New Zealand, 111
Nursing, 27, 33, 35, 40, 41, 82, 84
Nursing homes, *14*, 15, 32, 120

Paperwork, 18, 27, 69, 97, 107
Part-time workers, 12, 15-16, 51, 120-121
Peer review, 84
Perkins, Frances, 29
Physical therapy, 18, 50, 55

Play-or-pay plan, 109-110
Poor, 36, 37, 39, 44, 47, 79, 80, *81*, 82
Preexisting conditions, 13, 50, 55, 56
Preferred Provider Organizations (PPOs), 46, 101
Prescription drugs, 59, 67-69, 76
President's Commission on the Health Needs of the Nation (Magnuson Commission), 35
President's Commission on Mental Health, 44
Preventive care, 76, 120
Primary caregivers, 18, 37, 62, 63, 80
Private health insurance, 12, 35, 37, 44, 46, 51, 53-56, 60
Professional Standards Review Organizations (PSROs), 45
Prospective Payment System, 89-90
Psychiatric services, 32, 43
Public health departments, 28

Quality of health care, 23, 35, 49, 83-85, 111, 122

Rand Corporation's Health Insurance Experiment, 60
Rate setting, 89
Rationing of health care, 49, 77-79, 123-124

Reagan, Ronald, 46
Rehabilitation, 32, 120
Right-to-health-care issue, 19, 74-75
Roosevelt, Franklin D., 28, 29

Self-employment, 106
Single-payer plans, 106-109, 111
Small businesses, 12, 121-122
Social Security Act of 1935, 28, *29*, 30
Social Security Act of 1972, 59
Specialization, 40, 62-63

Tacrine, 68, 94
Truman, Harry S., 31, 33, 35, 39
Two-class system, 79-80, 82

Underinsured, 12, 51, 54-55
Unemployment, 44, 47, 51, 52, 121
Uninsured, 12, 51, 53-54, 91-92
Universal health care, 19, 30, 35, 39, 44-45, 48, 49, 74-75, 77, 79, 91, 92, 111, 121, 123
Unnecessary surgery, 65, 67

Working poor, 12, 13, 53
World War II, 31-33, 35

Xerox Corporation, 99